MW01252067

# THE GREAT HEIST

# THE GREAT HEIST

By Kenneth Del Vecchio

Published by Transit Publishing Inc.


ISBN: 978-1-926745-71-8

Cover design : Francois Turgeon
Text design and composition : Benjamin Roland

Cover photo :
© Corbis
© Destinations/Corbis

Backcover photo : © Destinations/Corbis



Transit Publishing Inc.
279 Sherbrooke Street West
Suite#305
Montréal, Quebec
H2X 1Y2
CANADA
Phone : + 1.514.273.0123
www.transitpublishing.com

Printed and Bounded in the United States of America

# DEDICATION

This novel is dedicated to a hero, Charles Durning. I have been honored to have this true gentleman act in several of my movies, and read the role of "General Early McAvoy" at a table read of *The Great Heist*. Charlie earned the Silver Star and two Purple Hearts for his courageous fighting and heroic efforts during World War II, in addition to being a 2-time Academy Award/4-time Golden Globe/9-time Emmy winner and nominee. The man thanks me every time I cast him in one of my films, but the true thanks is from me to him.

# One

There was nothing particularly special about the exterior design of the First American Bank in Rome. Certainly not the architecture. Though massive in size, it was, simply, a square. Your basic brick and mortar, with a few windows. The drab beige color scheme rounded out the plainness of this monetary holding cell.

Inside, *generally*, it was the same old thing. Tellers behind bullet-proof glass. Desks and chairs neatly laid out in a carefully normal floor plan. A few wastepaper baskets, phones, fax machines, and computers. Average Joes, or Giuseppes, filled out the mid-level managerial squadron. But, inside, it was just generally average.

Beyond the lobby furnishings, impenetrable glass, and the men and women who handled First American's day-to-day duties, was another structure…and another group of bank employees. This is where Christian Ranieri had planned to be for the last two years. He had worked ever so diligently to make it happen, utilizing influential contacts from four of the world's most powerful industries.

There was something exciting about being in this other, little known area of First American's Roman branch. Who was back there was interesting. How one got back there was more interesting. What was back there, though, was the most interesting.

Christian didn't just want to see what was in The Temple, the name given this special area by American bank executives stationed across the Atlantic. No, Christian wanted more. And, now, here he was in The Temple, getting more.

Surrounded by men with electrical, sound, construction, and various technical equipment, Christian sat silently in an empty corner of The Temple's outer unit, the first of three. He surveyed a room filled with precious pieces of metal and artistic creations, ranging from pre-Christ to just yesterday. There were original paintings from the great Italian masters. Some from France, Britain, Russia, Japan, and China as well. A sacred fifth century draft of the Bible, and some writings better suited for hell. This was Christian's vision. Godly on the one hand, Satanic on the other.

Here the colors were not bland. The walls were red and yellow and violet and orange. The ceilings, a rich chocolate black. And then there was the door. A perfect pink rectangle that led to The Temple's middle unit. Christian eyed it for a moment, and then another. He marveled at the knob, a platinum circle—real platinum. Then, he bypassed the men silently working their craft around him and walked to the door. No one bothered him as he turned the million-dollar knob and entered The Home of the High Priestess, a silly nickname for The Temple's second unit. The first unit had no nickname. The third and final unit, though, was known as nothing more than The Vault.

Once in The Home of the High Priestess, Christian met Serena, a voluptuous Swiss transplant who had nothing to do with the bank. With thick, straight, long blond hair, large blue eyes, proportionally larger breasts, and a perfectly toned five-foot-four-inch frame, Serena was the kind of woman that men noticed. Christian didn't, however, ignoring Serena's advance. Instead, he focused on the piles and piles of paper cash that covered nearly three-quarters of the room. Aside from Serena and one desk with a laptop, there was nothing else in the forest green Home of the High Priestess.

Christian knew that there were over two billion American dollars circling him as he departed this egg-shaped safe. Passing through a solid white drape, he arrived in The Vault. Here is where the greatest prizes were held. It was a fucking vessel of gold, Christian noted. Gold walls. Gold floor. Gold ceiling. And gold bricks. Side by side, one on top of another. Actual bricks of gold.

"Damn heavy, these bricks," Christian said to himself, as he picked one up.

"What?" Burt Walter, a handsomely chiseled forty-something American, asked his boss.

"Nothing," Christian replied, eyeballing the papers in Burt's hands. "So, give it to me."

Burt turned to Mario Leggetti, a twenty-five-year-old Italian native, who was no less attractive than his American counterpart. His muscular arms broke through the shoulders of his tight black T-shirt. He stood toe-to-toe with Burt, offering only an intent gaze. There was no sound. Not anywhere. Not in The Vault, or The Home of the High Priestess, or in Temple Unit One. Burt and Mario looked at each other, obviously ignoring Christian's presence.

"So, we're in," Burt began. His eyes, a deep shade of brown, moved from Mario to some of the gold around him. "As hard as it was to get here, it will be that much harder to get out."

"We leave the same way we came in," Mario smirked. His Italian accent was hardly noticeable.

"Shut up." Burt lit a cigarette.

Mario knew his statement was stupid. He lit his own cigarette, then walked to a large hole that had been freshly blasted in the far right corner of the room. At the very edge of the hole, and extending outward into The Vault, were steel tracks—a type not dissimilar to those that carried railway trains. Just smaller. There was about fifty feet of empty space on either side of the tracks. Ten large wheeled carts, connected to each other by brass rods, rested patiently on the steel grids.

Mario inhaled a drag of his smoke and turned back to Burt. "I'll get the others, and we'll start loading."

Burt nodded as he picked up a brick of gold. "Good. Get them. And let's clean this fucking place out!"

At that, Christian's pale blue eyes lightened. They shined above his overgrown beard that helped make the thirty-five-year-old look fifty. "Good! Perfect!" he exclaimed, as Mario whipped through the white drape.

Outside, in the bank lobby, it was business as usual. Checks were cashed, deposits made. Relatively small amounts of money handed back and forth. No one heard what was happening in The Temple. How could they? The Temple was separated from the teller area by the world's densest wall: a circular enclave of iron, steel, and brick, encased in the four-sided building.

Most First American employees didn't know The Temple existed. Their knowledge of what lay behind the teller zone was limited to a door that led to executive offices. Every weekday morning, at 8:00 a.m., the desk managers heard a faint buzzer. The tellers heard a loud buzzer because they were beyond the bulletproof glass. When the buzzer went off, Luigi Punto and Laney Maine went through that door and into the executive offices. Bank staff knew the pair as high-level management, with vice-president status. This wasn't exactly accurate.

Punto, with bristled white hair and a crinkled ruddy face, was nearing retirement after decades of glorious work in the banking business. Born and raised in nearby Naples, he was happy to finally serve professionally in his homeland. The chubby son of an auto mechanic, he was the first of the Puntos to attend university; he majored in finance. Prior to graduation, he had landed an intern position with a British conglomerate. For twenty-two years, Punto labored in Scotland, Wales, and England, only to be ultimately transferred to Australia. It was on that continent/country/island that Punto made his mark. For it was there that he met four-star United States General, Early McAvoy.

McAvoy had long since departed from his military career, shifting to an occupation that most closely resembled a political lobbyist. He consulted with an array of international oil, pharmaceutical, defense, and finance companies. Then he chatted with members of Congress and the military, which resulted in certain legislation being passed that benefited those McAvoy-consulted companies. In Australia, General McAvoy was aiding, more like creating, the launch of a new style bank. One that would never close, open twenty-four hours a day, seven days a week. The First American Bank.

Despite its name, this bank wouldn't be located only in the United States of America. This was to be the world's largest bank, with branches in every nation of North and South America and Europe. Australia as well, and many countries in Asia and Africa, would also house First American branches.

The General scooped up Punto and shipped him back to the British Isles. Changing employers, Punto spearheaded First American's interests in most of Europe, finally landing on the company's international board of trustees. This meant he could choose the destination for the golden years of his career. Punto chose First American's branch in Naples. General McAvoy, by then the bank's chairman of the board, instead ordered him to Rome—to oversee The Temple.

Laney Maine was a different story altogether. She was young, just thirty-two, and only seven years away from an Ivy League law school graduation. Simply, Maine was McAvoy's beautiful genius protégé. The General let her lead his business affairs without any reservation.

Now seventy-two, and fifteen years into the worldwide successes of First American, General McAvoy resided in the trendy Via Veneto neighborhood of Rome. His bank, only steps from his home, McAvoy visited daily. The base employees were honored to have First American's founder and chairman within their four walls. To them, he was a celebrity, and it gave those little people a wealth of pride to know that The General's favorite city was Rome.

As the lobby managers signed on new business and dealt with customer service issues, and the tellers exchanged euros and dollars, General McAvoy meandered in and out of the wooden executive door. Truly, he did love Rome. Oddly though, he never visited the Colosseum, walked the Spanish Steps, or threw a coin in Trevi Fountain. He did spend a lot of time at the Vatican, however. There, years earlier, he had negotiated First American's contract as the primary bank to safeguard the monetary and artistic assets of the Roman Catholic Church. Thus, the need for The Temple, The General's greatest joy.

Christian mulled the irony of Catholic artifacts and cash being warehoused in a place called The Temple. He didn't care, though, as he wasn't one for small talk—or thought. At this point, the massive money-house was flooded with light, and every member of his team was hurriedly carrying out his or her respective duties. Each man and woman had a distinct, personal task. All positions were unique, but equally important. This, no doubt, was a collaborative effort, which Christian clearly comprehended. He was the captain, however, and that role was unmistakable.

Several of the large wheeled carts were filled with bricks of gold. Four men and one woman were systematically piling the stash, with little chatter. Everyone else in The Vault quietly looked on. With the sixth cart full, Burt directed Mario and another younger man to push the first cart into the hole.

*Holy shit*, Christian thought, *what must The General think? The Vatican's gold being pushed through a hole in his vault!* So Christian turned to him, and suddenly yelled, "Cut!"

At that command, gaffers and grips began moving lights and various other pieces of equipment with names like jib arms, apple boxes, and C-stands. A Japanese man with the title of DP turned to two other men of Asian descent with titles of first and second AC, respectively, and asked them to move a 35mm camera. The best boy and his assistant pulled wires from the wall, and the boom operator asked everyone to quiet down again so he could get "room tone." This was all a confusing cacophony of technical undertakings that The General hardly understood, but it had been going on for several days now—and he had agreed to it. Making a Hollywood movie in The Temple was Laney's request, and she got the Vatican's consent.

"So let it be written, so let it be done," McAvoy stated in his never-lost commanding voice.

"But it's not all written," Christian replied, and pointed to his head.

"Oh?"

"Some of it is just up here." Christian turned from McAvoy to a plain Jane. "How long until the next setup?"

"Twenty minutes…maybe thirty," Plain Jane answered.

"Make it fifteen." Christian turned back to McAvoy, who was annoyed that anybody had spent half a minute speaking to someone other than him.

"This is the last day, Mr. Ranieri?"

"Yes." Christian spun around and grabbed one of the gaffers, a lighting guy. "Move the 4K maybe two feet…make it three!"

The gaffer nodded.

Christian to McAvoy, "Maybe one more day?"

McAvoy shook his head. "You've had your week, Mr. Ranieri. That's the contract."

"But to get it right, General—"

"No." The General began moving in a circle, physically mimicking his surroundings. "These are the world's greatest treasures…yes, you have put your sweat and tears into your project…but thousands, maybe millions, of other men have given their blood to obtain the riches that are in these three rooms."

Suddenly, from the foreground, a blurred body part reached through The General and touched Christian's cheek. A hand. A voice. "The martyrs who made this happen." Then a face. A beautiful face. Laney Maine.

Christian ignored The General again. "The first martyr?"

"Polycarp." Laney was now fully in front of The General. Three human beings, ranked in perfect symmetry: Christian, an inch from Laney, who was an inch from General McAvoy. Face to face to back.

"Who?" The General tried to get through the backside of his underling, Laney.

"The Bishop of Smyrna," Christian responded to Laney.

"And there have been so many others that died for His word." Laney was now almost lips-to-lips with Christian.

"I am aware." Christian moved that one measurement closer.

"Enough!" The General grabbed Laney by her shoulders, pulling her away from Christian before there was any actual contact. "Get your last scene shot…and by God, let's just hope that He doesn't think it is heresy!"

Christian nodded at The General and Laney with the slightest of smiles, and then drifted to a corner piled with gold bricks to revisit his plans for the ultimate scene to be shot in The Vault. The Love Scene. The greatest scene he had ever plotted, written, and directed. To be the greatest love scene of all time.

There had been many terrific fictional romances throughout the history of cinema, which had been made unforgettable by the most sensual of sexual encounters captured on film. The art of the love scene was not merely two actors simulating the rumble-tumbles of intercourse. No, it was much more, Christian knew. There were words that had been written, defining characters with meanings and motives, and back stories with wants and desires. And then there were actors, true actors, lending their personal passions and life experiences to the characters they were playing. And a production designer and art director, who collectively had created a set of longing, to be mixed with an illumination of the right light and sound. All to be brought to life on a medium of colorful, or perhaps colorless, film, under the direction of a master creator of fantasy lovemaking. Lovemaking that would stir the hearts of millions of moviegoers looking for that fantastic escape from their own reality. ..But Christian, as usual, wanted more. His love scene was going to be real. And his reality would have far more impact for audiences around the world than any past fictional love scene.

To create his reality, Christian had to overcome many obstacles. Not just the fifty or so crew members that were typically on set for the shooting of any given scene. Shooting in The Temple meant the presence of dozens of extra people who had nothing to do with filmmaking. It started, of course, with The General. But then there were at least ten other First American corporate leaders. And, more so, the security. There were armed, private First American security, Italian law enforcement, Italian military, American military, American CIA, and a group of unidentified men. Whispers had it that they were from the Vatican.

Everyone seemed pissed about the hole Christian's crew had put into the wall of The Vault. But, they all knew it was meaningless. Just a little cut, an abrasion that was much smaller than it would appear on the big screen. And it could be fixed in mere hours by First American's construction team. Christian mulled these matters, and others, for some time, and then concluded that he would carry out his final plans for The Vault.

He passed through the white drape from one money room to the other, and summoned the hot Swiss blonde, Serena Boll. She was the lead actress of *The Great Heist*, the movie at hand.

"You're ready, I suppose," Christian whispered, noting that this room was now filled with at least half of his crew and several of the armed muscle.

"I just have to disrobe." Serena double-blinked at her director, a signature gesture of this little-known actress whose first role was just a year earlier in Christian's cult hit, *The Seven Asses of Elka.*

Christian said nothing in reply to Serena; instead, he moved on to her would-be screen lover, A-list action favorite Burt Walter. The film's biggest star, Burt was always ready to remind Christian that he got him for a bargain at $2 million and five back-end points.

Before Christian could speak, Burt did. "What's my motivation for this scene? For screwing her in that vault of gold? I don't get it. I never got it."

Christian ran a hand through his thick locks of salt-and-pepper hair, an obvious reaction of frustration. "You like people to watch. You're a nut. Crazy…it's exhilarating to you that you're robbing over a billion dollars from the world's most safeguarded bank… and to fuck this hot bitch in front of your crew, while they're heisting the gold, is your own orgasmic masterpiece."

"Hmmm…that makes sense." Burt seemed to buy into the rationale. He folded up his sides—the four-page section of his script that contained this scene—and walked over to Serena, who was getting her makeup touched up. Without warning, Burt took her face and started what was intended to be a passionate kiss. But instead, Serena pulled back and pushed her palm into Burt's chin.

"Get the fuck off, Burt! You're messing my last looks!"

"How can I get into the moment!" Burt threw his sides at Christian. "There's a hundred people in here. No trailers. No damn dressing rooms. Makeup and craft service are in the same place…You got such a fucking bargain with me at two mil…and the leading lady is too good to rehearse!" Burt stormed through the drape and into The Vault. Hardly anyone noticed, already accustomed to hearing his star tantrums.

"That's some control you got over your actor." The General enjoyed what he determined was Christian's lack of leadership skills.

"I'm not concerned. I don't think what he has to do is something you need to rehearse."

Serena turned from the makeup artist. "No, baby, you're wrong. That man needs plenty of rehearsal to be with this woman." A double-blink. "Any woman, actually," referring to Burt's closeted homosexuality.

"Don't ask. Don't tell. Right, General?" Christian patted McAvoy on the shoulder and then disappeared through the white drape to pacify and further motivate his phony stud actor.

McAvoy watched him exit The Home of the High Priestess, and then walked over to Laney, who was standing with a man in a suit. "I'm not sure I like this director anymore. I'm giving him six hours to finish this scene."

"You know he's got a closed set," the man in the suit said.

"A closed what?" McAvoy snapped.

"A closed set, Early." Laney nudged closer with her own brand of sensuality. "It means that no one can go into The Vault because they're doing a love scene with nudity. Only the actors, director, and necessary crew…You agreed to it."

"I don't recall ever hearing about a closed set, Laney."

She moved in again, just as she did with Christian, putting her lips next to The General's. "You agreed…it has to be that way." She was very quiet with her words.

The General relented. "Oh…right…who cares…we'll be done in six hours anyway…and then I can have my Temple back."

"Right, Early. And we'll also have your baby, your perfect fortress, on thousands and thousands of movie screens all across the world." Her lips were now at his ear, her tongue brushing inside it as she spoke. "And no one will know where it is. A secret for everyone to marvel over, to be discussed at the water coolers and in the cafes and at the film schools...Where is First American's hidden temple? Where is General Early McAvoy's fantastic bastion of treasures?"

The General liked what he heard—and, no doubt, how he heard it. Initially he had expressed concern that the vast wealth being filmed in The Temple would be identified with the Vatican. But that issue had been negotiated away by allowing Christian to shoot only in the rooms with the cash and gold bricks. The public would know only that the riches seen in *The Great Heist* were indeed authentic, and held in one of First American's thousands of branches. That could be nearly anywhere in the world.

But First American executives knew that this didn't necessarily mean that those shooting in The Vault wouldn't open their mouths. Laney and the bank's lawyers, however, exacted contractual measures to ensure that the secret of The Temple's location would be preserved. Neither Christian nor his crew nor the studio funding *The Great Heist* could possibly afford to reveal the site of their shoot. For, how could they? The liquidated damages provision of their confidentiality agreements would bankrupt them all if they spoke the forbidden words of The Temple's mystical address.

A hint of mist arose from the floor around The Vault as Serena and Burt lay, completely naked, on the golden tiles.

Wang, the director of photography, crushed his right eye into the viewfinder of his camera, angling for the wide shot that would best present the strikingly gorgeous full-frontal nudity of these actors. Yasuhito, the first assistant cameraman, toiled with a knob on the camera, ensuring precise focus. The boom operator, Al, outstretched his arms, lifting the sound recording device up and outside the four corners of the 16x9 frame. The gaffer, Carmine, gave one last fidget to a hanging ball light, and the plain Jane first assistant director, Shelly, yelled, "Roll sound!"

A sound recordist beyond the drape responded, "Sound rolling!"

Shelley, cued, screamed, "Roll camera!"

Wang answered, "Rolling…camera set."

Then Christian, "Action!"

Serena climbed on top of Burt, passionately kissing him. Burt embraced her, driving his tongue in and out of her mouth, and then pulled her upward so he could kiss and fondle her bare breasts. Serena's hands traveled up and down Burt's body, stroking his ass and near his inner thigh. They rolled from one position to another, all the time moaning artificial, but believable, sounds of ecstasy.

Beyond the lovers, four other actors were blurred in the background, loading gold bricks into carts and pushing them out of the room. Their close-ups had been shot earlier in the day and the day before. Now they were relegated to ambiguous extras, hardly noticeable in the haze of Burt's and Serena's lovemaking.

Watching the monitor in The Home of the High Priestess, Laney, the other crew members, and several security operatives were all taken with the raw sexuality of the scene and the immeasurable brazenness of the stars making it while a grand theft was occurring around them.

Other than the calls to roll, no one spoke in either room, as Christian moved from shot to shot and angle to angle. The monitor went on and off in between takes, and the takes themselves went off without a hitch. Even The General was impressed with

Christian's style. He found it interesting that except for the first shot, the audience never again saw Burt's or Serena's faces. Just extreme close-ups of body parts, private and otherwise. The scene was largely sculpted out of sound—their moans in addition to the blasting and loading noises necessary for the story's great gold heist.

Hours passed, and the shooting and acting continued. There was no break for food, or even for the use of the restroom. Aware of the General's six-hour time limit, Christian was persistent, completing his task without interruption.

The General was relaxed, though, with Laney often having her lips close by, so he allowed the sixth hour to go by without complaint. Clearly, Christian was not finished. The General resolved to give the director some leeway on this last day of shooting in The Temple. Laney cuddled next to McAvoy, excited, watching the caressing movements of hands, the bouncing of breasts, and the gyration of pelvises, thighs, and buttocks. Her lips would touch The General's neck, ears, and cheeks, and she spoke measured carnal tones.

At the eighth hour, though, The General told Laney he had had enough.

When the monitor blanked to what seemed to be the one-thousandth new angle and take, he ripped open the drape and entered The Vault. For a moment, no one in The Home of the High Priestess heard anything.

Then, The General, in the calmest of voices said, "Holy mother of hell…he wasn't making a movie about stealing The Temple's gold…the fucker really stole it."

# Two

***One Year Later***

"The two most important words to me are *loyalty* and *reliability*. And in that fucking order."

Dylan Travant cock-looked the forty or so people at the three adjoined tables he had set up for his key crew and cast meeting. He was a man, with a boyish, yet sexy, round-cheeked face.

"If you're good to me, you'll get back one hundred times over. Not the same.. Not ten times better. One hundred times better." He sipped his whiskey from a rock glass. The ice had not yet started to melt. "If you fuck with me, though, I'll kill you… legally…meaning, I won't just hurt you back, I'll do everything I can to destroy you…Are we all on the same page?"

A moment of reverent silence. Then—heads started nodding and a few spoke words of *yes, of course,* and *absolutely*.

"Now, this doesn't mean I'm hard," Dylan continued. "Many of you know that. You've worked with me before." Back to the whiskey. A good sip. "I just want people who mean what they say, and say what they mean." The whiskey. "Michael." Dylan pointed to one in the crowd.

Michael, a gaffer with frizzy red hair and a burgeoning second chin, looked up.

"Michael, you started off as a production assistant with me, right?"

"Yeah. On *The Night House*," he answered, referring to one of Dylan's previous movies.

"At $50 a day…and now you're making a hell of a lot more than that, right? And about a half dozen films to your credit."

Michael nudged his own glass of liquor as a modest toast to Dylan. "Seven of your films. You're why I'm here in the business."

Dylan surveyed the whole group. "On every movie I generally have three to four assholes…But ninety percent, we work out well. Do your fucking job. Do it well, as we agreed upon…And we'll all make some bucks together."

"But you'll make the most!" a black guy, third table down, second seat, yelled.

"You're fired," Dylan responded, no emotion, cold eyes.

Silence.

More silence.

Then the black man started laughing, low at first, then a hearty laugh. A few more in the room joined in. Others looked around, not sure. Then Dylan smiled and started laughing himself. "Okay…that's Lincoln…my DP. He says what he wants or my film doesn't look good." Whiskey again. "And he's right…I make the most money—by far." Whiskey glass smashed to the table. "And I fucking deserve it!"

Everyone joined into the laughter.

"Drink! Drink!" Dylan screamed. His wonderful blue eyes gleamed like no one else's in the room. A director, every ounce as handsome as his star actors…but much more powerful than any of them.

A pig —Andy—bucked in a cage of mud and straw. Two others joined him. The second and third were Peg and Sandy. American names. Just like the thirty or so others that the Italian man owned.

Luigi Punto was now finally retired from First American Bank, and the banking business altogether. He had a monstrous estate just seven miles outside Naples, his birthplace. He was a favorite son of the city, donating euros anywhere he could. Churches first, of course. Veterans' organizations. Hospitals. Disease control centers. Orphanages. Research groups. Scholarship funds. To private families. To everyone and anyone that suited his liking.

And Punto built a farm. Something he always wanted, right from childhood. He had cows, chickens, ducks, sheep. But more than any of them, he had pigs.

Punto wouldn't eat pork. One would think he was a Muslim or a Jew. But he was a Catholic, weather-worn for sure, by the theft of so much of his Church's wealth.

Back to the pigs. Punto wouldn't eat them because he loved them. They were smart. Smarter than his dogs, he proclaimed. So there would be no chops or bacon or ham for him.

And now he observed Andy and the others in the dirty, hay-filled pen. A cigar languished, smoking on its own, from the tip of his lips…lips…lips…how he loved lips…lips…those goddamn lips…*her* lips!

"Luigi," the lips purred. "Luigi."

Punto refused to turn from his position, which was in front of the lips.

"Luigi."

He knew the voice. He knew the lips. He didn't need to turn around to determine the identity.

"Luigi."

The cigar fell from Punto's mouth and into the pig crib, igniting a bale of hay.

"Luigi."

Flames licked at the hay…Punto not moving.

"Luigi." The lips were closer now.

Punto motionless. Flames rising. Andy bucking.

The lips were ever so close. "Luigi."

Andy screaming…the flames burning rapidly…the other pigs squealing in unison…Punto holding fast.

The lips now touching the bristled white hairs of his naked neck. "Luigi."

Flames burning all around him, his pigs screaming in the ecstasy of a fiery dance. Punto suddenly spun around to meet the mouth of a cast-iron corpse-maker. One blast into his brain, and the Naples philanthropist was as dead as his pork-barreled friends beside him.

The eighth reporter raised her hand. Not unusual. There were thirty-nine others with their hands raised as well. Dylan just had them categorized by numbers. The eighth woman was in the eighth seat from his left, in the front row. So she was Number Eight. There were ten seats in this leading row, as in the several rows behind it. But reporters were in the first five only. Then, fans and other fillers of sorts. A typical press conference, with dozens of still photographers blinking shots, and moving picture cameras simultaneously synching reality on video and film. Man, he loved it! Dylan wasn't camera-shy, though his only role in filmmaking was behind the lens.

He wanted to answer the question about to be posed by Reporter Number Eight. True, he had no idea what she was going to ask, and no reason to think she was going to pose any special question. It was just something in the way she looked. Dylan was honest with himself—she was fucking hot. Cropped, perfect brown hair, just long enough that it fell to shoulder level.

Electrifying eyes…and a smile…a smile he didn't normally see from the press.

"Yes, Number Eight."

The reporters looked around, having no knowledge of Dylan's number scheme.

"I mean you." Dylan pointed directly at his four-plus-four number.

The woman spoke up. "This film definitely seems like it would be your chance at critical acclaim."

That was a shot to the heart. Dylan was known as the king director of the action heroes, not for anything cinematically important.

"You're hitting social issues. Abortion. The death penalty. Health care," she went on, either oblivious or uncaring of the daggers she was driving. "But what about *The Great Heist*?"

*What about it?* The look on Dylan's face said everything. Fuck, hadn't he heard enough yet! This had been going on for the last ten months. No one had really accused him of anything. But it was he—Dylan Travant—who had brought Christian Ranieri into the world of Hollywood pictures. He kept hearing the same questions: *Who was Christian Ranieri? How did you meet him? Where did he come from? What excited you so much about a short film he did on Greek gods that you recommended him for a small, three-picture studio deal? And wasn't it you who recommended him to the newly deceased Luigi Punto, to shoot the cornerstone pieces of his third feature at The Temple?* Everything was now out in the open.

"What about it?" Dylan answered.

"Just wondering why you didn't make a movie about the whole thing…Seemed like you knew a lot," the hot brunette bitch inquired.

"Well, Burt Walter knew a lot more…and I guess that's why he made a movie about it," reminding the audience of Walter's directorial debut flop, a docudrama about his experiences in the making of *The Great Heist.*

The press conference ended with "Hmmm" from the puckered lips of the hot brunette bitch, Reporter Number Eight.

The White House. It was white. No matter the amount of time that had passed…the outside of it was white. No chipped paint showing underlying color. No dust to darken it. Certainly, no graffiti to brighten it.

The President was also white. A sickeningly pale milky shade…rather gross. But Jesus, so tough…And she was the first woman president.

"You can come in," The President offered.

A woman entered.

"And?"

"We have him, Madam President."

"I'm not so confident."

The other woman, a lot younger, was nervous. To no one else. But to The President, yes, she was nervous. And she had already let her Commander in Chief down. "Yes, Madam President. Please be confident. I have him. I'm sure."

The President sipped a rock glass of ice and scotch. She eyed the lips of the woman in front of her. "You better be, Laney."

# THREE

“I was hog-tied. You know, my hands to my feet. More like shackled. And a banana was stuffed in my mouth.”

“A banana?” an off-beat male interviewer asked.

“Yeah, a freakin’ banana. A piece of fruit.”

“Oh, that must have been dreadful,” the interviewer coddled.

“Yes. It was difficult…having something so big and so long stuffed down my throat.”

“Could you breathe?” The interviewer was quite sympathetic.

“Yes…but barely.”

“Oh my…I…” the interviewer grabbed the hand in front of him. He might even have been smitten with his subject. “Please… if you can…tell us more…”

“No,” the subject said, “Just watch…It’s a re-enactment.”

“Okay.”

Cut to:

Inside The Vault…or someplace loosely designed to look like it. Burt Walter is tied up on the golden floor. His mouth stuffed with the yellow fruit he had just described moments earlier. He is tied from extremity to extremity—by tight, yellow rope. His eyes tell the scene around him.

A beautiful blond bombshell, an actress playing Serena Boll, pulls her fully nude body from her in-scene lover. Her breasts and brow, coated with sweet sweat, spray sexually moist droppings upon her similarly naked partner. The moment she departs, in-vault cast and crew descend upon him. Burt's momentary cries cannot be heard, drowned out by the wall-blasting all around him. It's unbelievable: Christian Ranieri and a small group of actors and movie professionals are stealing what may be the greatest riches of the world.

Christian was indeed shooting a love scene. There were unclothed actors. There was passion. There were many takes. But after the first few, all filmmaking stopped. Thus, the banana-stuffing and rope-tying of Burt Walter. The other actors and crew—really thieves—were blasting much deeper into the circular First American Bank fortress safe. So deep that they met a tunnel that Christian and his team had dug months prior.

Inside The Home of the High Priestess, however, General McAvoy, Laney Maine, First American security, American and Italian law enforcement and intelligence, and several unnamed Vatican overseers saw something much different. What they witnessed—on the monitor—was a year-long planned and executed pre-recording of nude body parts, noise and voices yelling words of moviemaking: *rolling, set,* and *cut*! They were stupefied by classic cinematic artistry, sucked in by their own most innate, raw instinct—lust. All the while, though, Christian was beating the world's greatest security system, heisting hundreds of millions of dollars of ancient, and not-so-ancient, gold assets.

"Cut the projector," the real time Burt yelled out. He rose from a plush red chair that he had specifically ordered for this event, a seminar-style film-festival screening of his box office bomb.

"You see, everyone in that vault was in on it, except me."

"Not you, Burt!" a fan yelled out from the audience.

"No…not me." Burt's ass was in the interviewer's face, who was seated in his own plush red chair.

"You chose an interesting approach to tell your account of *The Great Heist*," the interviewer began, excited by Burt's backside. "Part documentary. Part feature. With you playing yourself…The whole process had to be difficult."

Burt turned around, his crotch now near the commentator's mouth.

"It was trying…emotional…reliving it was dangerous for me." Burt reached to a table for a water pitcher.

"Jesus Christ, how fantastically stupid," Dylan whispered to Janice, an actress of clean-cut American looks who was starring in his upcoming film, *The Catch.* They were both sitting in the back of the audience, present at the film festival as part of a pre-production publicity junket arranged by the studio.

"No, it's sad," the actress whispered back. "I want to hear the rest."

Dylan smirked.

Burt began again. "Some think Christian Ranieri was brilliant. I think he was just a criminal."

"Can you help us get into his twisted mind?" The interviewer held Burt's hand for the second time.

"No…I can't be in that mind…I can just tell you what he did…because I was there" That line was a cue to the projectionist to start rolling again.

Burt is now squirming on the gold tiles, roped up with the banana. His penis flapping around with his contorted movements. Serena has pulled on a black spandex dress, and she's working furiously with the other members of the crew, loading the last of the gold bricks into the wheeled carts.

Burt looks up from the floor, helpless and frightened. He eyeballs a computer hard drive and monitor that is simulcasting naked bodies making love on a golden floor, with a blurred backdrop of men, equipment, and gold something. This is what all the others were also watching in the adjoining Home of the High Priestess—hundreds of takes of a sex/theft scene that Christian had shot ninety days earlier in a room designed to look like The Vault.

Inside the hole in the wall are three of Christian's team, racing carts of gold through a dimly lit tunnel. At the tunnel's end, there is one man, Burt's screen partner, Italian actor and career thief Mario Leggetti. With an electronic elevator of sorts, Mario mechanically lifts the gold bricks to the surface. As they bubble through an opening in the ground, Christian directs three other men to load them into a waiting box truck.

"Cut the projector! Please, cut it!" Burt was upset. His eyes teared.

Dylan rose from his seat. "That's it. I've heard enough. The idiot wasn't hurt…And though his movie sucks, he's made a killing telling this story." Dylan continued to speak to Janice, not bothering to maintain a whisper. "Book deal. Interviews. Speaking tour. DVD sales." Heads turned as Dylan left the theater, rambling on about the monetary perks obtained by Burt Walter through *The Great Heist.* "Bullshit!"

The door slammed behind him, and Burt kept telling his tale of woe, his microphoned voice echoing through the cracks of the wooden barrier.

"Popcorn. Extra butter." Dylan said, with no oral break from his profane utterances.

"So do you want an all-American snack or cattle excrement?"

Dylan turned from the popcorn stand to the recognizable female voice that came from behind him. It was Reporter Number Eight, the hot brunette bitch. Her hair was much darker up close, almost black.

"You're not here for that crap inside, are you?" Dylan asked Number Eight.

"No."

*She has some fucking lips.* "Oh." Dylan didn't know what to say.

"So is it the popcorn or the bullshit? You seem to be enraptured with both."

Slice to:

A bed with a king-plus-size mattress. Rose petals spread across the sheets, trickling to the floor and across the fifty-yard room. Not high ceilings—the highest. No skylight. Instead, five synchronized stainless steel fans cooled a room that also, of course, had central air. A two hundred-inch plasma screen, playing one of a thousand movies from a private hard drive. Furniture? Yeah, sure—from 1800s Spain, 1600s England, 1492 America, and pre-1000 Italy. This was Dylan's bedroom. But he was fucking Number Eight in a tiny bathroom off the front door of his home. The two couldn't wait to get carnal.

"Put it"...Pump…"Put it"...Pump… "Put"…Pump… "Please…Dylan…put…"

"Shut up, Number Eight. Keep it sweet." Dylan pumped.

"I'm not sweet." She glistened with heat.

"I know…you fucking bitch." Dylan pumped harder. Harder. Harder. Over the toilet top. Over the bowl. Harder. Harder. And then—a collapse.

Number Eight rolled in the rose petals, thinking. Nude as she had been in the absolutely otherwise never used tenth bathroom of the Travant house. It was the most accessible closed-door room once inside the entrance to the North Jersey mansion. But now who cared about that latrine. The two had finally made it to the master bedroom, and Number Eight was frolicking in the flowers. Dylan was brushing his teeth in the master bath.

"Dylan," Number Eight held one of the red petals over her left tit. "How come you only made one movie in the last two years?"

Teeth brushing. Eyeballing Number Eight's naked ass in the mirror. No answer.

"Your buddy," she glanced at Dylan from her mirror purview, "Christian… Ranieri…he made four to your one…and then started *The Great Heist.*"

Dylan spit. The mirror reflected Number Eight's nice tits, one completely showing, the other half-covered with flowers. And then her stupid inquisitive look. Still no answer.

"So you introduced Christian to Hollywood. He was a nobody with only a film festival short." She dropped the rose petal, revealing both of her shapely C-cup breasts. "You know, it's kind of odd. Him in. Then you out. And he used a lot of your actors…and studio connections." Number Eight's short strip of bush appeared in the mirror as she stood. Dylan watched her at a mirror angle as she reached into her purse.

He entered his bedroom, holding a towel at his side. It was rather bunched up, in his fist, not flowing freely as all else was. "I thought we were fucking. Not interviewing."

Number Eight lifted a few of the blood love leaves and met Dylan near an authentic Christopher Columbus hand-me-down worth a half-million dollars. Her pocketbook was clenched in her other hand. "You know, I lied to her."

Dylan moved forward.

"I told her I was positive." Number Eight's hand dug into her purse.

Dylan moved closer.

"But I wasn't positive…That is, until I saw…and felt…your piece."

*Oh shit. This bitch is hot. Naked and knowledgeable.*

Dylan stepped in closer.

Number Eight ripped an object from her bag. A gold brick. "Now I am positive. And I can't lie to The President…Dylan

Travant." Gold at tit level. "You are…Christian Ranieri. And you forgot one fucking brick!"

Dylan rushed at Number Eight, but it was too late. She cracked the million-dollar slab against his forehead. Not a spray of gold dust, but real human blood gushed from the side of the director's head.

Dylan, nude, staggered back.

Number Eight, naked, rushed forward, preparing to swing again. But before she could—

"Drop the brick, you fucking cunt!" Serena, in a one-piece white summer dress, fashioned a long firearm in Number Eight's ear. She had appeared, seemingly, out of nowhere.

Momentum and adrenaline rolling, Number Eight bounced forward, toward Dylan. Serena shot her in the chest, though, before she could move more than a quarter step.

"Cool." Dylan dropped to his knees. "That couldn't have killed her, right?"

"How could it?" Serena responded, annoyed. She had used nothing but a stun gun; it wasn't a lethal shot.

"Just worried because it was close range." Dylan pulled a towel over his cock and ass.

Serena went over to one of the super-expensive dressers, opened a drawer, and pulled out an average-priced pair of blue jeans. "We should've killed Laney back in Rome." She pointed to Number Eight's everything-but-lifeless body.

Serena threw Dylan/Christian the jeans.

"We don't ever kill Laney." His words were solemn, monotone. He pulled on the jeans and then bent down to his naked attacker, kissing her forehead. "We won't ever kill you…Just keep trying to figure it out." Fresh blood dripped from his matted, crushed hair onto Laney's uncovered chest and face.

# FOUR

*"A tunnel!"*

The President sipped scotch from a newly poured glass, then continued. "There was a tunnel that ran from the man's bedroom to a road in New York State? That's over five miles...And there were motorcycle tracks the entire way?...That man had a goddamned hidden passage, from death's door to eternal safety?"

Eyeballing Laney, The President took another sip. "Now let me get this straight. He takes you out—top CIA! And poof! He's gone on a motorcycle before fifty agents arrive at this New York City suburb McMansion. And no one can trail him! The United States government can't find this…this…movie director!"

Laney observed, waiting to see if it was her turn to speak. The President drank, while Laney thought…

It was all a little hazed, dark, cloudy, whatever the fuck you want to call it, but Laney knew exactly what happened. Serena wasn't an actress…okay, maybe she was for about two years…no, she was *playing* an actress. Christian Ranieri trained….fuck that, Dylan Travant trained her…he handpicked her from somewhere. Certainly not the United States. The bitch had a foreign accent.

Dylan had created more, though. He had created Christian Ranieri. Dylan Travant, the ultimate green screen-blue screen, mystery-morphing director had initiated, formulated, cultivated—maybe cloned—this entirely new filmmaker. Alright, perhaps he didn't *clone* him. But, bottom line, he *was* him. Laney was sure of that. In fact, Dylan wasn't even denying it at this point. There was word he was holed up in an anti-United States South American country, ballsy, and ready to shoot his current project.

The circumstantial evidence proving the Dylan/Christian masquerade was compelling, going well past their obvious "relationship." Every time Dylan was around, Christian wasn't. When Christian was making a movie, Dylan was on sabbatical. The one time Dylan made a movie, Christian was in Kenya prepping a shoot, beyond media probe.

Their movies, though different—Dylan's adventure-action, Christian's film noir—had distinct, similar dialogue and themes. Dylan had contacted Luigi Punto, his longtime First American Bank contact and financing partner, to help Christian obtain the necessary permission to shoot at their Rome branch, in The Home of the High Priestess and The Vault. But fuck, this wasn't enough. Something else sealed it for her.

It was his cock. It was so damn big. Laney knew, because she had fucked both Christian and Dylan. But more than that, it was so thick. And then…there was a star tattooed on the head. Goddamn proof positive! Christian was Dylan. Period.

"Speak up, my precious asset." The President had comsumed enough of her scotch.

"He's in South America…I think Venezuela."

"I think you may be a little off." The President picked out an ice cube. "Tell Laney what we know."

Light flashed from nowhere into a sixty-something man's dark, dark eyes. "He's not in Venezuela. He's in Chile." This was The Defense Secretary. He knew.

"Okay. Chile…I'll go there," Laney offered.

"No," The Defense Secretary ordered.

"No," The President affirmed. "No…go to your boyfriend. We have a lot of fences to mend with him…and his father, The General."

Laney acquiesced, and then began to rise from the White House couch.

"You are a slut—you know that, Laney." The President revisited her scotch, "Thank you."

Laney nodded, and then left her Commander in Chief.

If Mitch McAvoy had a beard, there surely would have been icicles clinging to it. Instead, his beet-red face acknowledged the sub-zero weather he was enduring. How he loved the cold. This and hot peppers, he knew, kept wrinkles from appearing on his perfectly sculpted forty-year-old face. "Fuck Botox. That's for phonies."

"What?" Mitch's cross-county companion Justin Keller asked, trying to catch up to the faster, physically stronger man.

Mitch plowed ahead, not answering Keller, nor slowing down for him. This was pretty much how he treated the senior senator on Capitol Hill as well.

"Fifteen years!" Keller yelled. "Fifteen years, Mitch! I'm—" Gasp! "I'm fifteen goddamn years older than—"Gasp…gasp again! "—you!" Keller collapsed by a rock.

Mitch, no longer hearing gasps or bitching, turned around. Lifting his goggles, he witnessed Keller kneeling in the snow. The fifty-five-year-old waved one of his ski poles at Florida's junior senator. "You wait for me, you son of a bitch!"

Mitch observed Keller for another moment, then replaced his goggles. He trotted farther off into the white ice, allowing the senior senator's curses to fade out with the progression of his graceful Arctic strides.

Age was not the reason that kept Early McAvoy from cross-country skiing on the ice caps of Greenland. The General worked out daily, bench-pressing more than his own two-hundred pound weight, and curling with men who were only three to four decades old. Nor did his absence on the frozen trails have anything to do with fear of frostbite or other weather-based dangers. In war, he had killed men in colder terrain. Simply, The General had no interest in this sort of exercise, and instead of joining his son outside, he enjoyed the heat of an inside hotel lounge with Laney. Just Laney. The General had arranged for the lounge, and its companion restaurant, to be closed for the balance of the day, wherein only his private guests could partake of the fine dining and top-shelf alcoholic beverages of Greenland's most notable hotel.

"I thought we were going to have a little party in here, Early." Laney pawed at his navy blue cashmere sweater.

The General ignored her, puffing on a pipe stuffed with apple tobacco. He was still consuming his surroundings, a habit of necessity that he had learned in his military training. *This was some place*, he thought. It was interesting to The General that he thought this, because the man was rarely impressed. But this hotel was something.

The restaurant had no walls, only windows. Each plank of glass was forty feet in height. Tables were neatly arranged in a circle around the outer edges of the restaurant and lounge. A rectangular bar, live cooking station, and cashier unit lined the inset of the high-class eatery. And a fish tank, filled with not only exotics but also with varied species of salt-water sharks, was crafted along the entire side opposite the forty-foot windows. Hotel management was in a constant state of fish replacement because the larger were always attacking and eating the smaller. *Just like humans*, The General pondered.

"I was thinking about my former employee, Luigi." The General inhaled some apple into his cheeks. "It's unfortunate," he looked at Laney, "his untimely passing."

"Yes, unfortunate, Early." Laney had no pipe, but she sipped the vice of a California cabernet. "But he was disloyal."

"That's the truth. He was disloyal…still, what a bizarre way to go…burning in flames with all those pigs." The General delivered a wave of smoke in Laney's vicinity. "Pass me a bread stick."

Laney grabbed a tray that was closer to The General than to her, and picked out a hard sesame stick. She handed it to her boyfriend's father, who also, at a time, was her boss and then some. "I thought we were having a party here." Laney tried to get back to where she was before.

No response. Just pipe smoking.

"It's beautiful in here, General." She dropped the first-name use. "But what does this country have to offer? It's kind of boring."

The General drew in some more apple, savored it for a moment, and then blew it out. "Not so boring to the United States of America…your country…your President…the one you work so hard for."

There was a lot to The General's words, Laney understood. The reason that Mitch and a number of other members of Congress were visiting Greenland was because a very strong arm of the country's government was lobbying the U.S. to purchase it. They wanted Greenland to be the fifty-first state, leapfrogging Puerto Rico, which seemed content remaining a commonwealth.

Shit, some Puerto Ricans even wanted to secede and leave the world's greatest democracy altogether. That was a powerful Greenland argument, and one that The President was clearly listening to. So she dispatched Mitch first. The junior Florida senator had a penchant for traveling and he certainly liked adventure. He had arrived two weeks before the balance of the ten-person envoy, presumably to initiate in-person negotiations. Instead, though, Mitch was ice fishing, skiing, and building igloos. Laney laughed to herself, thinking about the few cell-phone conference calls Mitch possibly allotted the Greenland leadership… Greenland…Greenland…Greenland…. The General's words alluded to more than The President's thoughts of Greenland. His references to "your President" and "the one you work so hard for" were a jab, no doubt, about her role in bringing in Christian Ranieri to shoot *The Great Heist.*

The General, here and there, intimated that Laney's true allegiance was to The President, and not to him and First American. "After all," he once proclaimed, "you really are just a government operative, assigned to me, to protect the intermingling crossed lines among my bank and the several nations it serves…most of all, our beloved republic."

Laney thought The General believed either that she was negligent in not ascertaining Christian's true intentions because she cared little about his bank, or that she turned a blind eye to a coup that benefited The President's administration, or, even more so, that The President herself was behind the theft. Now, she thought, would be a good time to dispel that ridiculous paranoia. The revelation about Dylan Travant would have great meaning.

"General."

"Laney," a voice even harder than The General's was behind her, "Laney, turn around and give me a fucking kiss."

Mitch! Laney spun around, and without any more provocation, began a several-minute intimate kiss. His lips were enjoyed by this woman as much as he delighted in hers. The cold of the man's mouth was filled with the warmth of hers. An erection, seemingly impossible given the travels he just completed, came in full force. *Nowhere near as large as Christian/Dylan's*, Laney privately conceded, *but Mitch can work it much better.* He was the true lovemaking artist. For her, this was love.

With one last rapture of the tongue, Mitch ripped back Laney's head. "Tell me about that fucking zero Dylan Travant."

The General puffed on the apple tobacco. Laney eased the release of her hair and head from Mitch's grasp. Really, he let her go.

"What about…Dylan Travant?" *Fucking asshole. This takes away from my revealing it... Maybe he doesn't know everything.*

"I know everything…so does my father." Mitch unzipped his down ski jacket. He always preferred down for the coldest weather.

Laney looked at The General, who was still smoking. Then back to Mitch. "What do you know?"

"I know you were visiting a lot with him. Why?" The jacket was removed.

*Maybe he just thinks I fucked him. Maybe I can still reveal that Dylan is Christian.* Advising a general and senator of the successes of her work was more important to Laney than her boyfriend conjecturing infidelity. "Christian Ranieri is Dylan Travant!" There, she let it out.

"What!" Mitch dropped his jacket to the floor.

*Yes, he just thought I was cheating!* "Yeah, it's confirmed…I confirmed it. Why do you think—"

Clapping. Pipe down in an ashtray…and clapping. No speaking. Just clapping by The General. Here was the party Laney had asked about. Only three people, but there was liquor, sex, smoking…and clapping.

"So is he in Guantanamo?" The General finally spoke.

"No." Laney picked up Mitch's jacket.

"Another military prison?"

"No."

"A federal prison?" The General watched Laney's inaction. "I guess he's not in a state institution either. Those damn insurance companies are never going to stop busting my balls."

"The Vatican was paid off, you saw to that right away—"

"Yes, but that doesn't mean I'm still not bothered by them."

The General bypassed his pipe, and instead took a drink from Laney's wine glass. "Where is he, Laney?"

"We—"

"He's in South America." Mitch finally re-involved himself in the conversation, taking Laney's hand. "I'm sorry, I thought something else was going on."

Laney ignored the second part of his statement. "How do you know he's in South America?"

"Because I'm sure you know how well I know Dylan. I know where he would go."

"If it wasn't for you, we would've never had that…that Christian…Dylan…whoever the fuck he is…at The Temple. You introduced him to Laney in the first place." The General placed Laney's cabernet back on the table.

"I never introduced anyone to Laney," Mitch defended himself. "Right, Laney?"

"That's true, General," Laney answered.

"No, you're right." The General, for some reason calmer now, maybe because of the wine, picked up his pipe again. "You introduced Christian to Luigi Punto."

"No, Dad. You're still wrong. I introduced Dylan to Luigi… and then, years later, Dylan introduced Christian to Luigi…I never even met Christian Ranieri."

"Mitch, didn't you just hear the lady? Dylan is Christian." Smoke in…smoke out. "Either way, your little fondness of Hollywood and writers and directors and movie stars brought this thieving, conniving asshole into my bank…and my treasures."

"So this is my fault?" Mitch asked of his father.

No response. Just smoke again…and a smug look.

"It's Luigi Punto's fault. He's the one who betrayed your father…And you." Laney tried to remedy his hurt.

"No. Dylan betrayed me." Mitch pointed to his chest. "Stealing from my family…from me." Mitch called to a woman outside of the three-person party. "Guinness."

The bartender acknowledged him and opened a cooler in the center aisle.

"How did he pull this off?" Mitch continued. "Aside from the obvious makeup and acting job…I mean, you did background checks on Christian Ranieri. He was a real person. I read the fucking reports."

The bartender came over with the dark Irish beer and handed it to Mitch.

"He obviously assumed a dead man's identity…someone of little consequence." The General knew the game. "Who would think? Because no one had a reason to believe he wasn't real."

"Of course not. He had a résumé. A list of public successes in his critically acclaimed art house movies. Several actors and producers and critics to vouch for him," Mitch finished his father's correct thoughts.

"Christian Ranieri—the actual Christian Ranieri—dropped out of a California high school in the tenth grade." Laney looked at Mitch and The General to see if she should go on. Confirming eye contact, she continued. "His father, he never knew. His mother died a few years later. No one remembered much about him. Just that he was a drug addict, in and out of rehabs for over a dozen years. We now know that he didn't rebound and begin making short films in the hills outside L.A. Those were little movies made by Dylan playing Christian. The best we can figure out is that the real Christian Ranieri is either strung out somewhere or dead of an overdose that no one learned about."

"Someone learned about it." Mitch dragged down the last of his Guinness. "Another junkie. Dylan Travant."

"Dylan's a drug addict?" Laney seemed concerned.

"Not much of a secret."

"You should know," The General kicked in.

"I've never touched a goddamn drug in my life." Mitch wasn't shy in answering back to his father.

"Was it heroin? Did he shoot up?" Laney returned to Dylan's drug use.

"You seem awfully concerned." Mitch pointed to his glass, notifying the bartender that he wanted another. "No…he did a lot of hallucinogens like LSD and a bunch of prescription painkillers…the fucking loser almost OD'ed himself once… that's where he probably found the poor Mr. Ranieri. Who knows, maybe he killed Ranieri himself." Mitch decided to save the bartender a trip and fetch his beer in the middle of the room. There, he sat by himself and drank. The General smoked. And Laney thought about Dylan Travant.

This man wasn't a mystery like Christian Ranieri. And the revelation of his involvement certainly would erase any McAvoy thoughts that the CIA, The President, and/or her administration were entangled with *The Great Heist.* Dylan Travant obviously had the wherewithal—and the connections—to pull off an inside job. He and Mitch knew each other since their late teens. Dylan was a freshman at Columbia University when Mitch was a senior. They both came from privileged families. Dylan's were New Yorkers, with mom, dad and grandparents on both sides entrenched in the entertainment industry. Mitch, of course, was the son of a war hero, the greatest of modern-day battlefield leaders.

Their friendship was on-again, off again, primarily rooted in Dylan's inner love-hate relationship with his older college mentor. Mitch had a perfect 4.0 grade point average. And he was an incredible wrestler, significantly better than his Ivy League teammates. He was the school's athletic leader from sophomore year on. Stronger than everyone else. Faster. More skilled. But, above all, more powerful. And he was charming. Younger or older, they all looked up to Mitch McAvoy.

In Mitch's fourth and final year, Dylan joined the team. Tough for a first year, but he was a mere sparring partner for Mitch. A great high school wrestler, Dylan had a hard time dealing with the beatings. And he suffered, watching Mitch score one hot upper-class cheerleader, athlete, and academic after another. Dylan wasn't satisfied with all the gorgeous freshmen on his trail; he wanted more.

In a year, though, Mitch was gone from Columbia University and attending Georgetown Law. Dylan reveled in the last three years of his collegiate career, just about equaling Mitch in varsity wrestling victories—and victories with the women. When Dylan graduated from Columbia, Mitch graduated Georgetown. Their friendship, though, had never ceased; it ignited at this graduation juncture.

Dylan immediately ventured into film directing.

Mitch, the born leader, however, wasn't ready to lead. He practiced, sometimes, in the field of law as a criminal defense attorney—never losing—and then dabbled in the movies. Producing. Acting. Financing. Whatever. For three years, he hit movie sets, coming and going as he pleased. If he acted, it would be only three to four days at a time, never more than a week. As a producer, he watched when he wanted, and gave orders when he wanted as well. As a financier, or really the one who raised the money, he simply instituted demands, all of which were carried out. Again, this privately irritated Dylan who, as a director, was on set every second of every shot of every movie he made. Similarly, he was intimately involved in every moment of pre-production and post-production.

Both young men succeeded. Dylan was quickly touted by the studios as a fierce action/adventure director whose films earned significant revenue. Mitch picked up the nickname "The Man with the Midas Touch" because every movie he embraced ended up in the year's top twenty grossers. Most of these films were directed by Dylan.

During this cinematic tenure, The General was cleverly pushing Mitch toward his real calling—as a political leader. He barely acknowledged his son's movie experiences, meeting Dylan not more than a handful of times. But he did set the boys up with several power meetings and parties. These were events that lacked any entertainment luster. But they were full of people with political and financial influence.

Thus evolved the courtship of Dylan Travant and Luigi Punto. Mitch arranged for Punto to finance a martial arts-airplane hijacking movie, written and directed by his younger friend. The movie grossed over $100 million; accordingly, Punto kept raising funds for Dylan. Not surprisingly, the pair continued making money together, even more so after Mitch bowed out of the business for his first congressional run. The General gave only a cursory review of the Dylan-Punto partnership. Why should he care if they made money together? Mitch was done with the movie world and prospering in the field of his true calling. As a political leader.

Years passed, and Mitch rarely, if ever, communicated with his college teammate/ filmmaking buddy. By the time Punto came to The General and Laney with the Temple-shooting request of Christian Ranieri—an ally filmmaker of Punto's partner, Dylan Travant—Mitch was a U.S. senator.

Laney knew neither Dylan nor Christian, but Christian had the highest of recommendations. The lot, of course, included Dylan and Punto, and also several other top movie execs, financial barons, and political leaders. Even Mitch had said, "If he's a friend of Dylan Travant's, then he's a friend of ours."

# FIVE

It was warm for a November afternoon in Baltimore. Especially by the water. There was a light breeze, but it wasn't noticeable to the hundreds of crabbers who lined piers and docks with varied metal cages stuffed with chicken and fish. Nor did the drizzled rain seem to bother the fishermen, professional or amateur. The sun showers had come and gone all morning, and the day seemed destined to become brighter.

Mario Leggetti preferred a hook with a raw piece of duck attached to it, rather than the cages used by most of the other crabbers. He claimed this was an old Italian recipe for snagging the best of the salt water, clawed creatures. With a quick whip of his left arm, a nylon string with hook and poultry sailed a few hundred feet into the bay. "Watch this," Mario told a bald sixty-something pier regular.

"Watch what, Blondie?" the bald man inquired, seeing nothing special in Mario's line toss.

"You're an American?" Mario tugged on his nylon.

"*Si*, I am, Blondie." He pointed up and down the pier. "I'd say ninety percent of us are."

"Well, you are about to witness what no American can do. Only what a trained fisherman from—"

"Italy?" Baldy interjected.

"Yes, how did you know I am from Italy?"

"Come on, Blondie." The bald Baltimore man started hoisting up his cage. "You are the actor—or is it thief—Mario Leggetti." The cage surfaced with several crabs in it.

"Old man by the sea." Mario stepped closer. "What does that mean to you?"

The cage was now on the wooden dock they shared. The bald man opened it, showing hardly any fear after outing Mario. "I just want an autograph." He reached into his flannel coat. "For my daughter."

Mario grabbed the man's hand, feeling inside the coat. Only a pen rested inside the garment. Mario pulled it out, and scribbled several sentences on the flap of a box of bait. He handed it to his crabbing partner. "When you pull in my line, take the very large crabs on the hook and follow the recipe on the box." Mario started to walk away. "Some fine virgin olive oil, salt, pepper, and scallions. It's from my grandpa. A true Italian artist in the kitchen." At that, Mario kissed his fingers as a sign of good-bye and jogged off into the bright sunlight of the afternoon.

Senator Keller was a glutton for punishment. His own fault, for sure. He didn't have to join Mitch in his frolics in the snow. There was no matter of national security at hand. No budgetary or economic issue waiting to be resolved. Not a single U.S. interest being discussed. Not even a pet bill hanging in the balance. No, Mitch just banged on Keller's hotel room door from five minutes before sunrise until five minutes after. The senior senator accompanied Mitch just to stop the harassment.

Now, here he was on some mountaintop he couldn't name. In full ski gear and clothing. These slopes weren't akin to the bunny trails he was used to traveling in upstate New York or New England—and even some of those were tough for him to navigate. No, this Greenland mountain range was altogether different. It was a fucking nightmare.

"Ah, Mitch, I'm out of my league here." Keller decided to make his last pitch before his snowmobile guides left them to ski down the treacherous paths that lay ahead.

"Nope."

"What do you mean, 'nope'?" The engines of the vehicles that could take Keller back to safety were running.

"I mean, nope."

Keller began walking toward the snowmobiles. "No, Mitch, I'm sorry. This one I'm not—"

Gunfire!

"Get down, Senator!" Mitch dove on top of Keller, taking him to the ground. As he did, a bullet ripped through Mitch's down coat, blood almost simultaneously spraying through his freshly torn sleeve.

The snowmobile operators, really Secret Service, began shooting into the sky. A helicopter above laced shots back. As the two armed forces exchanged fire, Mitch lifted Keller from the ground, maneuvering the older man onto his back as if he were a knapsack. He crushed a ski pole into the ground and initiated an assault down the mountain.

Blood splattered from Mitch's shoulder and into Keller's face as the younger man dug into the snow to increase speed.

"Mitch!"

"Don't worry, Senator," Mitch turned his head back, "we'll be safer going through those trees."

With the additional weight of Keller on his back, Mitch soared from the normal ski path into a wooded area.

"Mitch, you're shot!" Keller grabbed tightly onto his savior's back.

Responding to Keller was no longer a priority. The gun-toting helicopter had veered off from the American agents and was now following Mitch's trail into the trees, firing randomly but nonstop into the wilderness. Mitch could hear the engines of the snowmobiles that were attempting to track the senators' route. Their only job, and objective, was to protect the men they were serving. Die trying, if it was necessary.

The green. The green. Mitch was exhilarated. The green of the trees. All of them were green. Clean, crystal icicles. Frozen brown bark. And white, white snow. Now sprinkled with tiny, perfect droplets of Mitch's red. The fearless could survive. Know your colors. Know your environment. Know your enemy. The fearless, as he was, tore the goggles and heavy hat from his head, so he could better feel the cold and become a part of his surroundings.

He couldn't hear the motor sounds now. Nor Keller's cries. There was just trees, weather, and ground…and occasionally bullets. Mitch raced in and out of thirty-, forty-, and fifty-foot plant growths, maneuvering against terrific odds. A wrong cut in one direction, at any given second, meant instant impact. And impact, at their speed and gravity, meant death. But departing from this forest of green also meant death. So Mitch traveled onward.

With the afternoon, the breeze in the Baltimore area had picked up. Same for neighboring Washington, D.C., where Mario Leggetti had just arrived. Realizing a change in hair color alone was not enough of a cover, he added shades to his repertoire. Black-rimmed with dark lenses, the glasses were a fine complement to his tanned skin and bleached flock.

Girls were screaming, boys too. And women and men. Fortunately, their yells weren't for the fallen actor, otherwise his arrest would have immediately followed. The hollering, instead, was for The President. It was a campaign year and, although unopposed in her party's primary, she still needed to gladhand and make speeches. Even though the general election was nearly a year in the future.

There was a western theme to this day's event. Lots of cowboys, rodeo types, and their accompanying gal pals. The event was put together by several Texas congressmen and one of the state's two U.S. senators. A $1000 ticket bought the holder chicken and rib barbecue, heaping portions of steak, lots of live country music, and a personal appearance from the headliner, The President herself. All in a fenced-off outdoor greenery just a stone's throw, okay, several throws, from the White House.

Leggetti bypassed the entire affair, pedaling by on a bicycle, with a long package strapped across his back. In the distance, he heard some second-rate lady band, the Sexie Dicks or something, introduce The President. Then, fainter, he heard some microphoned chatter about abortion, affirmative action, gay marriage…and even fainter about universal health care, wars of some measure, and good ol' economics. There seemed to be some talk of how the country was being uplifted by the current administration from a recession, depression, or the sort.

Leggetti parked his two-wheeled vehicle in front of a six-story brick building, where books for the academic world were printed and sold. As he chained his bike to a street sign, two reporters that he recognized approached. Truly, this would be no meeting of happenstance. Leggetti was waiting for them.

"The fine white bitch, Karina Kelly." Leggetti touched his shades. "And her sidewinding partner, Boppin' Bob Barkstone."

"What?" Barkstone, a snooty Capitol reporter, wasn't used to the slap talk.

Leggetti ignored him. "You are a cutie in person, Karina." Leggetti slung his long package over his shoulder.

"Where would you see me 'not in person'?" Karina observed Leggetti and his bike. "I'm a newspaper columnist, and you obviously know that, Mr. Blond Bicycle Man."

"Let's go, Karina." Barkstone had determined this chitchat to be a complete waste of time.

"Hold on, Boppin' Bob." Leggetti reached into his pocket, pulled out a small red envelope, and handed it to Karina. "Just a little note. Get to it when you can. I'm sure you'll be busy with The President's profound speech." Over on the stage she was now talking about the history of the cowboy and how it related to American culture.

"Thank you, Blondie." Karina took the envelope, started off with Barkstone, then turned back. "You still didn't tell me how you recognized me."

"Your picture." Leggetti had reached the door of the book building. "It's next to your column." He smiled and walked through the door.

Karina, apparently satisfied, continued toward The President with her newspaper colleague. "He looked familiar too, didn't he, Bob?"

"Never saw him before." Barkstone concentrated on The President.

So did Leggetti. Taking the stairs two at a time, he ascended six flights to the structure's highest floor. There lay the company's retail store where the academic public purchased books of biology, chemistry, economics, math, and titles from other, more specialized undergraduate and graduate disciplines. As he reached to open the door to floor six, a man in khaki slacks and a button-down shirt exited. "Hey!" He startled Leggetti. "Everyone's taking the stairs today!"

Leggetti looked down the empty stairwell, "Yeah," and attempted to walk past the man, whom he mentally tagged to be a political science professor.

"Returning something? Some audio visual aids?" The "professor" was intent on making Saturday afternoon conversation.

"This?" Leggetti tugged the brown-paper-wrapped package hanging from his shoulder. "Curtain rods." He finally nudged past the man.

"Curtain rods? Oh." The man, content with the few words exchanged, headed down the stairs.

Leggetti meandered to a shelf of books arranged in alphabetical order by the author's last name. He plucked out a thick one about criminal statutes and flipped through a few pages, stopping to read a couple of lines about the writer's Renaissance-Man background. Then he placed the 1000-pager back on the shelf and proceeded to the restroom. It was time to take care of some personal business.

Outside, a group of Texas political leaders congregated around The President on a stage that was roped off like a boxing ring. The backdrop was a cleverly styled montage of images characteristic of the Lone Star State, The President's homeland. Cattle, skyscrapers, and oil wells, with colorfully printed city names, San Antonio, Dallas, and Houston, and the smaller towns of Alamo, Coldspring, and Fredricksburg. Directly behind The President were photographs of people. Old, young, middle aged. Some were fair-colored, some dark, others in between.

Texas Senator J.W. Wayne addressed the pride of Texas. "Madam President, it is my honor…my pleasure…to give you the ultimate symbol of the cowboy." A Marlboro-looking man himself, Wayne produced a cowboy hat and, with a wide grin, affixed it upon The President's head.

As The President returned to the microphone, with her own brand of grin, Leggetti swung open the sixth-floor restroom window. His brown-paper package now unwrapped, the blond

Italian conducted the few necessary mechanical maneuvers to fire his 6.5 x 52 mm Carcano M981/38 bolt-action rifle.

The sound unmistakable. The screams began instantaneously.

His first bullet hit its mark, the top of The President's recently-gifted cowboy hat, causing it to fly fifty feet above her head. The President's milk-white skin soured into skim as she shoved aside her press secretary, and sought cowardly cover at the feet of several Secret Service agents.

More screams and a second shot. A direct hit to the midair hat. As the ultimate cowboy symbol sailed further with the breeze, Leggetti fired off three more bullets. The hats of multiple cowgirls and boys blew with the wind, at varied altitudes and in north, south, east, and of course, west directions.

Heads turned every which way but loose, looking to see where the shots came from. Several Secret Service agents rushed The President to a black sedan and hurriedly transported their Commander in Chief to safety. Other agents, along with D.C. police, rattled excited utterances over electronic headsets and cell phones.

*Where the fuck was the shooter?*

"There!" A woman in a ruby power suit screamed, pointing to a blond man in shades running on the rooftop of the academic book building. He was still carrying the rifle. Law enforcement aimed their weapons, but couldn't shoot at him. There were workers on the roof.

Leggetti darted by the stunned blue collars and grabbed an out-of-place rope that hung from some scaffolding. The workers had wondered, earlier in the day, why it was there. Their questions were answered as Leggetti used it to swing from one rooftop to another. A mixture of gasps and cheers accompanied his landing, as well as the first shots fired at him. But then, poof…he was gone.

With Leggetti's disappearing act, Karina Kelly ripped open the red envelope and read the three lines scribbled on the white card inside: *Give this to Laney Maine – CIA. Tell the President to contact Dylan Travant about the moon. See www.moonrudeandnude.com.*

Karina handed the card to Barkstone. "I told you he looked familiar."

The daylight in the Greenland mountains ceased as quickly as Mario Leggetti had escaped Secret Service capture. And just as there was no longer any political gunfire in Washington, there was none in the Arctic forest. In fact, there was no sound at all, except the fierce wind and the crackling of a fire that Mitch had ignited. The fire, though, could not be seen by any being, human or animal. Mitch had burrowed deep into the snow, building a temporary igloo shelter. The walls and ceiling were several inches thick and frozen solid, not susceptible to melting by the perfectly centered flames. Smoke was channeled through a hole in the ice cap, which acted as a chimney. The dark mist merely blended with the night.

Senator Keller was cold, much colder than Mitch. The pair's clothes had been soaked by the snowfall that began about an hour into their wooded trek. It became particularly heavy when the downhill skiing ended, and a cross-country march commenced. Mitch, though bleeding, had demanded continual travel, acknowledging to Keller that if they weren't found or couldn't find civilization by nightfall, their chances of survival would sharply decrease. Keller knew his partner was a realist, and was gravely concerned with their current location.

Mitch, shaking from the beginnings of frostbite, unzipped Keller's jacket. "All of your clothes have to come off, Justin."

"Mitch," Keller's teeth chattered as he spoke, "Mitch…I don't…like…you…that much."

"I don't like you at all, Justin." He pulled off the jacket and then the man's pants.

Keller cascaded off into a hearty laugh as Mitch helped him remove the balance of his clothing. His teeth clanking all the while, he asked, "Are we—" chatter, "going to—" chatter, chatter, "have to—"

"Spit it out, Justin."

"Hug naked together?" The senator laughed the rest out.

"You mean use our body heat to keep warm—and alive?" Mitch took off his own jacket and looked at the shivering, naked older man. "Yes, Senator."

Mitch removed all else and grabbed hold of Keller as he slipped into an undesired nudity.

The men's clothes were placed as close to the fire as their bodies. As they waited for their clothes to unfreeze and dry out, the senators hung on to each other, listening to the sounds of the godly yellow burnt offerings, and the hellacious white and blue of their cold.

Keller instinctually clasped one of his hands over Mitch's bleeding shoulder, providing whatever pressure he could muster.

Mitch gently removed his hand. "It's only a flesh wound."

"How do you…know?" Keller was warming up a bit and could now speak for longer clips without much interference from his chattering teeth.

Mitch reached across Keller's back, cupping his own right hand over the wounded left shoulder. "I just know."

The situation was awkward. Words were necessary to help time pass. And Keller, never at a loss for words, wanted to keep talking. He was frightened and embarrassed, but he didn't want to speak about that. He wanted to feel, somehow, normal. So, the topic would be politics. "Mitch, I have a bill, the Keller-Kingman bill—"

"What?"

"Keller-Kingman bill—" momentary teeth chatter, "to eliminate eminent domain except in…"

"Except in cases where local, county, and state government all agree by at least two-thirds vote." Mitch rubbed up and down Keller's right side, utilizing the friction to increase body heat. He continued in the discourse to avoid thinking of their physical contact. "You have my vote."

"Tell me, Mitch," Keller rubbed back, pleased with the conversation and relieved by the fact that their penises never touched, "Do you want to purchase this country?"

Mitch's eyes electrified with the flames of the fire that now somewhat comfortably heated their ice home. "Yes."

Keller suddenly jumped back with a distant new noise. "Did you hear that?"

"Dogs!" Mitch jumped up and yanked his half-dried pants from the ground. Keller also went for his clothes.

"Here! Here! We're in here!" they screamed, simultaneously dressing.

The barking came closer. As it neared, Mitch blasted through their life-giving shelter. Keller followed. In moments, they could see beams of approaching light.

"Mitch!" Keller re-grabbed his fellow Florida senator, knowing their harrowing experience was about to end. "I was dead if you left me…You will be on that ticket. You will be the next Vice President."

Electrified eyes. "Maybe."

# SIX

The Defense Secretary was wrong. So was Laney. Dylan Travant wasn't in Chile, or Venezuela. He was somewhere in cyberspace, with only an internet address.

But his film crew was in a South American country. A nation in the pubescent stages of wealth, supported by an Eastern European bloc. New Nicaraguan leadership hardly cared that the United States government didn't want this movie made. With French financing, the American studios couldn't be pressured into stopping production. Nicaragua argued no involvement.

Nicaragua's prime minister did promise, however, that Dylan Travant or Mario Leggetti or any of the known participants in *The Great Heist* would be arrested if they set foot on Nicaraguan soil. Furthermore, he would immediately extradite them to the United States. None of them was in his country, the prime minister told U.S. officials. So there was nothing he could do.

Indeed Dylan was on the Nicaraguan set every day of shooting—via a computer monitor.

All of this seriously pissed off The President. So she scribbled. On a chalkboard. Her scribbling was fast and therefore hard to read. She didn't care. She was The President. Let them learn to read it. The scribbling continued. And continued. And continued. Much longer than usual, they all thought. And the screeching of the chalk was definitely abnormal. Always annoying, this time it was deafening.

"Here it is." The President finally spun the chalkboard around, revealing her long scribbled list. She liked to put things in writing, but didn't want to have a record of it. Thus, her tools—chalkboard, chalk, and eraser. Laney, The Defense Secretary, and The Secretary of State read her list as best they could. The handwriting was atrocious.

After several moments, The President started to become irritated. It was evident in the creases in her cheeks; the Botox had not been a success. The cheeks still wrinkled, and they were her dead giveaway. Never her eyes. Not her smile, or lack thereof. And not her brow. It was those goddamn cheeks. The woman couldn't hide her anger. Someone needed to speak up immediately. But it wouldn't be Laney. She was too nervous. And it couldn't be The Secretary of State. She was too weak. That left The Defense Secretary.

*Fuck it, I'll tell her.* "Madam President."

"Yes?" Cheeks subsiding.

"I can't read your list." The Defense Secretary stood up and referenced the green board. "It's too sloppy."

Cheeks creased to the maximum. "What? It's obvious what it says. You two can read it, can't you?" She put out a hand to Laney and The Secretary of State.

Neither answered.

"Madam President," The Defense Secretary started.

"It's clear what I wrote." The President was absurdly adamant.

"Madam President, simply, we can't read it." He shifted his eyes to the other two for support. No help from either.

"Fuck it!" The President rattled off the list.

*Mario Leggetti*

*Dylan Travant*

*The Moon*
*Mitch McAvoy*
*The Vice President*
*The Vice Presidency*
*Karina Kelly*

"Now do you get it?" The President flipped the chalkboard back over. Now there was only blank green in front of her audience…and blank faces. She swung the board back to her list. "How about Ms. Kelly?"

"I can handle her." Laney was confident.

"Can you? How?" asked The Secretary of State. Once Laney had spoken, that allowed The Secretary of State to get into the action. Wedged between Laney and The President in age and status, it was easy for her to question Laney. "This little reporter is causing a nightmare for us. Those moon articles are making our administration look inept."

"Her articles don't make The President look inept." The dark, dark eyes of The Defense Secretary chilled the women around him. "They make every administration going back to Nixon look inept." The man wore his sixty-five years well. Like The President, he had the wisdom of experience. Unlike her, he had no wrinkles, and no corrective surgery that made it that way. Just good genes. "We haven't been to the moon since 1972. Do the math. That's nearly four decades and how many presidential terms? But I think I know what your concern is, Madam President."

"You do. I made it an issue. I said I would be the one that would take our country to the moon again." She snapped a finger at her scribbled list, specifically *The Moon.* "Russia and China, Christ, even Israel and Japan are promising their people that they're taking them to the moon. This can turn into a public relations disaster."

"Worse," The Defense Secretary interjected. "It will make them appear technologically more advanced than us. More so, the perception that they are stronger than us."

The Secretary of State let out a slight laugh. "Even more so—the perception that they actually went to the moon."

The President's cheeks wrinkled, and then went red. "You shut your mouth." She turned to the youngest woman in the room. "Laney, please leave us."

"Should she?" The Defense Secretary asked.

The green and white of the chalkboard stung with immediate pain; more the white than the green. The words described power, status quo, change, strength, weakness, winning, losing, and hypocrisy. The green, it just represented wealth to The President. The green always mattered. For that, and the parts of the white that had grave importance to her, the President asked herself, *Should Laney be advised? Could she help? Was Laney the asset that she had groomed her to be?* "Laney, sit back down. Listen to him."

The President poured a rock glass full of scotch. No ice. And then The Defense Secretary revealed the mystery of the moon.

Neither the United States, nor any human being, had ever set foot on the tiny planet-of-sorts that orbited with the earth. It was all a well planned and well executed political hoax. Designed to deceive other nations, their leaders, and their citizens more than America's own. The international climate in the sixties was dangerous. The Soviet Union and the United States battled in a cold war. Everything was on the line. Democracy versus Communism. President versus Prime Minister. Control of other countries. Nuclear weaponry. The power of national defense. The power of the economy. All issues were substantial and magnified. Space travel was not lost in the shuffle. In fact, it emerged as the symbol of strength. As the symbol for winning. Who was scientifically more advanced? The United States of America or Russia? Who had the economic wherewithal to make it to the moon? Who had the resources? Who had the courage?

The answers to those questions translated into the answer to the ultimate question—who was truly the world's leader?

So each superpower embarked on a quest to land its flag on the moon first. Scientists and astronauts were engaged. The solar system, galaxy, and space in general were explored. And millions upon millions upon millions of dollars were spent. There was one problem, however. It was scientifically impossible for a human being to get to the moon. Any who tried would surely die!

"Excuse me?" Laney cut into The Defense Secretary's story.

He looked to The President, who offered an answer. "Yes, Laney. We have never been to the moon. We had a brilliant president who orchestrated a wonderful short movie with some very talented filmmakers." She sipped her scotch as a matter of course. "We're talking about one of—not *the*—but one of the most classified and little-known fictitious excerpts of our history."

Laney couldn't control her thoughts or questions. "Does Mitch know? The General?"

"This was exactly my fear." The Secretary of State responded instead of The President.

The President ignored her third-in-command. She walked over to Laney and performed her greatest act of affection. She touched Laney's hair. "No, my dear, they don't." Cheeks, perfectly rosy. "And they won't ever...Because your loyalty is with— who?"

Laney stood from her seat to face The President eye to eye. "You."

The lips. The President was satisfied. But she stood, captivated. The lips. Her hand touched Laney's hair again. The lips.

"Madam President." The Defense Secretary decided that things needed to move on.

The President shifted her attention from the lips. "This brings us to Dylan Travant." No more affection. "You understand where he comes in?"

Karina's nipples shined brightly through her damp bathing suit. The bright red one-piece wasn't totally wet on the top, because she had been wading around in only waist-deep water for the last twenty minutes. Either way, *her lights are on,* Barkstone creepily thought. *What tits.* Barkstone offered his partner a towel as she ascended from the pool. *She's too hot to be a writer.* His pornographic thoughts transcended to political words. "Mitch McAvoy is going to be her Vice President." *I've got no balls.* Barkstone's penis was hard, but instead he spoke about government.

Karina bypassed the towel and, fully frontally, squeezed out whatever $H_2O$ juice remained in her hair. What pain this was for Barkstone, a forty-something geek with the perfect fat-skinny body: no muscle, so not too much body weight, but lots of flab and gelatin-like components.

"That seems to be the writing on the wall." Karina held her place in front of Barkstone, never reaching for the towel or even her clothes, which sat in a chair only a few feet away. "What a perk." She referenced the indoor pool that was part of the health club membership their newspaper provide, in an attempt to compensate for the paltry salary they were paid.

"Yeah, it's Disney World." Barkstone was prepared to melt—or force himself upon her —at any moment. "Keller's already publicly said it. He's muscle. He pulls The President's fundraising strings. The Vice President is out. She hates him. This is the move. McAvoy's young, smart, from a great family…and he's a freaking hero." Barkstone wiped unnecessary sweat from his face. "The Vice President is out."

"Is he?" Karina brushed a thumb across her hard-nippled breast as she took the towel from Barkstone's ever waiting hand.

"The Vice President isn't out."

The President erased *Vice President, Dylan Travant, Mario Leggetti, Karina Kelly,* and *The Moon* from the chalkboard.

"Is it that we can't afford to lose such a fine political veteran from the ticket?" She sipped her scotch. "A man of principles… values…who is ever so dearly loved by the people." Scotch. "My people?" Scotch. "What do you think?" The President beckoned her Secretary of State.

"I—"

"It's a rhetorical question." The President refilled her glass. She was becoming intoxicated. "The Vice President is a moron. Handpicked by the national chairman, super delegates, and all the other bright lights who thought we should have a balanced ticket." A hearty sip of the scotch. "If they want a balanced ticket by the fact that his stupidity would offset my intelligence, then they did good."

"Madam President," The Defense Secretary interrupted and pointed to the remaining item on her chalkboard list, "Mitch McAvoy, our fine junior senator from Florida."

"Florida? Ha!" She smashed her empty rock glass down on the table, already finished with that round. "The man's a northerner." She was referring to the state of Mitch's final high school stop and the home of his Ivy League college. Truly, though, he was a military child, a vagabond who grew up in multiple locales. "Now that would be a balanced ticket. What do you say?"

"I thought we agreed that we were dumping the mental midget from Kansas." The Defense Secretary meant The Vice President. "And replacing him with Keller's life jacket," meaning Mitch.

"Yes, the hero." The President started her umpteenth scotch. "While I was knocking down my press secretary on her fat ass to avoid Billy the Kid's target-shooting circus, young Mr. McAvoy was halfway around the world, bleeding, carrying the country's most influential statesman on his back." There just wasn't enough scotch in her current bottle, so she opened a new one. "*Patriotism in the Arctic: Boy Wonder McAvoy Saves Life, Saves Greenland*

*Purchase.* That was some headline." The President hated every Karina Kelly article. "My headline *President Loses Hat, Saves Self,*" she picked up the actual newspaper, "*Sharpshooter Makes Daring Escape in Dodge City.*" The President stared at the newspaper, and waited for someone to say something…anything.

Laney, though in the mix of everything, felt like she knew nothing. With her Commander in Chief's drunkenness came the possibility that she wouldn't remember half of the meeting, so Laney gathered some courage from The President's liquor. "The two of you can make the greatest of headlines together." *Holy shit, she hasn't stopped me.* "With you putting the final touches on the Greenland purchase…and your record in ending the war… and Mitch's brilliant health care plan that you can sign into law… and the United States going back to the moon, a—"

The President smashed her glass into the chalkboard, the amber of the scotch dribbling over Mitch's scribbled name, partially erasing it. "The McAvoys know nothing about the moon! They're outsiders." The President made a beeline to Laney, in perfect step, not an intoxicated hobble. She stroked the younger lady's hair again. The Defense Secretary and Secretary of State tepidly watched. "The McAvoys, like ninety-nine point nine, nine, nine percent of America, think that we've already been to the moon." Hair fondled. "The General was a mid-level officer when Nixon's coup went down. He rose through the ranks as a wartime commander, not a mind at NASA, nor a foreign policy wonk." She let Laney's hair go with one hand, but then picked it up with the other. "And Mitch, he's in the same boat with ninety-seven of his other Capitol bench-warmers."

"Does Senator Keller know?" Laney felt comfortable, for some reason, within The President's touch.

"No." The dark, dark eyes were back in the discussion. "Keller does not know. But I thought Mitch should be brought in. He could be valuable. He has experiences." The Defense Secretary looked at his President.

She relinquished Laney's hair. "What you will see is a perpetuation of what is already there."

"What's that?" the only man in the room asked.

"The General thinks that I ordered down the U.S. military from the outer perimeter of First American's Roman branch… from his Temple…Thus, allowing Christian Ranieri, or this fucking Dylan Travant, to steal the Vatican's gold…"

"Did you?" The man was bold.

"Wouldn't you know?"

The Defense Secretary eyed her.

"He doesn't trust me." The President turned to Laney. "Nor you, my blackest of widows…Because you came to him from me. Do you know what that means?"

Laney looked on, offering no response because she knew what her boss wanted.

"It means that Mitch doesn't trust you either. " The President stroked Laney's hair one last time. "And that's why I am telling you what he hasn't…I will be having a primary, with Mitch McAvoy running for president against me. " She let Laney's hair go. "Not with me."

# SEVEN

Karina traded in her one-piece bathing suit for a two-piece business suit. A shapely black, knee-length skirt, topped by a matching fitted jacket. Her pink, spandex tank top accentuated her substantial breasts, but was largely covered by the three-button jacket.

As a reporter, Karina rarely dressed so professionally. The business simply didn't call for it. The restaurant where she was dining with Senator Mitch McAvoy did. Barkstone similarly attempted to meet the Senator in style. He failed miserably, however, wearing a cheap light blue suit with a black paisley tie and brown loafers that didn't match. In short, he looked like a dick. In sharp contrast, the maitre d' fitted nicely into a $1500 handmade silk suit. He greeted the writers at an oversized marble desk with a practiced smile.

"Reservations, sir?"

"Yes. With Senator McAvoy."

Karina momentarily envisioned the man dancing on the desk with a top hat and cane. But Mitch spotted the pair from afar, interrupting her daydream by waving them over to his table.

"Go ahead," the maitre d' offered, as they walked past him, ignoring his small stage of authority.

*So we didn't land on the moon in 1969, or go back in the early 70s.* Laney mulled over the proposition—the fact. *Jesus Christ, it was all a fucking hoax to win the great space race. None if it was real. The moon buggy rides. The rocks. Al Shepard's silly golfing. Neil Armstrong's historic giant leap for mankind. It was all a bunch of bullshit!*

*Think about it,* The Defense Secretary had told her. *One piece of common sense alone tells you. Why haven't we gone back? If we really, truly had the ability to go to the moon, we would have covered every square inch of that gigantic rock. We would have ravaged it for every possible resource. We would have a goddamn colony up there by now, with supermarkets, houses, gas stations, and strip clubs. Does it make sense that we put our men in rocket ships and sent them to the moon only during the Nixon administration? And then never again? Not in over thirty-five years? When our technology has increased...how much?...Oh, maybe a billion times.*

Laney switched on her computer, prepared to follow The President's orders. The hard drive warmed. Laney wrestled with the scientific evidence proving the moon hoax. She needed to know and understand it all in order to carry out The President's most crucial task. The same mistakes couldn't be made twice.

"The corn here is incredible." Mitch passed a family-style dish to Barkstone.

"The corn, Senator?" Barkstone took a heaping portion, then passed it to Karina.

"Yeah. It's called Firehouse Corn with Bacon." Mitch took the first bite. "Incredible."

Barkstone followed. "Wow. Delicious."

"It is." Karina was already into her second forkful.

Mitch cut into his porterhouse steak. "First, several tablespoons of olive oil are heated in a skillet at an extreme temperature. Red hot. Then, fresh corn, from the cob, is added. Salt, pepper and lots of butter are added. Sauté it for a few minutes, mixing in the butter with the corn, olive oil, and spices." Mitch sipped a smooth California cabernet from a large wine glass, noting his dinner companions' enjoyment of the corn as its recipe was betrayed. "Next, you add blue cheese. Then sprinkle fresh dill into the pan."

"How much?" Barkstone asked, mixing the corn with his steak.

"Just enough." Mitch looked at Karina. "Always, just enough…Then finally, when it is done," Mitch scooped up a spoonful of Firehouse Corn with Bacon, "drizzle in bacon grease, only a little. Stir in a sizeable portion of bacon pieces…and eat." The senator put the spoon in his mouth.

"The man knows the recipe so well because he created it." The General came out of nowhere.

Karina and Barkstone stood from their seats.

"Please, sit down." The General glared at his son "You didn't see *him* stand up."

"A pleasure, General McAvoy." Barkstone shook the General's hand. They had never met.

"General McAvoy," Karina blushed, "it's too much to be with both of you at once."

"You, Ms. Kelly, are an angel." The General kissed her cheek.

Mitch continued to eat, not paying any attention to the introductions. "So my father took away the surprise. " Mitch washed down another piece of steak with the wine. "I am the chef."

"I thought there was a bigger, more important surprise. That's really what we're here for, right?" Barkstone was aloof, arrogant.

He had no wealth, no military rank, and no elected office. But he had influence. As did Karina. The power of the pen, and the press.

"In due time, my friend," The General spoke with substantially more power. "Eat some more corn."

Barkstone dug into his dish.

*You almost died at my hand. Then again, I nearly died at yours. You were good, Laney. I figured you as Reporter Number Eight. Not Laney Maine, First American Executive. Or really CIA*

Laney was on Dylan's website, one specifically designed for her. One that only she could access, via the web address provided to her from Karina Kelly's red-enveloped card. The note she was reading was the home page.

*You were hot as a black-haired brunette reporter. Is it appropriate to call someone with black hair a brunette? In any case, you indeed fooled me. I thought I was just nailing some sexy reporter...But, as we both learned, we were making love to a lover...Someone we had already traded intimacy with. You, with Christian Ranieri. Me, with, well, a First American CIA operative.*

*Do you think Karina Kelly read this before you did?*

*Did the star on my cock give me away?*

*Who was a better lay—Christian or Dylan?*

*Do you want to get inside? Get somewhere that Karina couldn't, even if she inappropriately read this web page. Yes, Karina, I'm mocking you. You can't get where Laney is about to go, because I'm not inviting you. Back to you, Laney. Here's how you proceed:*

*Inside The Vault, in the far right corner, there were gold bricks. Truly, there WERE...Once I removed them, however, what lay there?*

Laney immediately typed the answer: *Alexander Hamilton.*

Seconds passed, then: *Correct. The General's hero.*

A new web page opened. *We are here to talk about the moon, space travel, and such. But let's first talk a little more about you, me—and Mitch McAvoy.*

Laney was glad she was alone. Against protocol, against the CIA director's wishes, but not The President's, she was visiting Dylan Travant's site without any other agents present. Nothing was lost, though, as all information was being captured, and in every technological manner possible. At this point, things were certainly personal.

*Look, you've sucked my cock and, albeit unknowingly, mine again as Christian. But then, you've sucked Mitch's as well. First question—whose cock tastes better?*

Pause.

*You can't proceed unless you answer...And, Laney, you must answer correctly.*

Laney went to the key pad. She typed: *Yours.*

The screen flipped. *Wrong.*

"Wrong!" Laney blasted her own computer.

She thought, and then typed a second answer: *Mitch.*

The page spun in several different directions. Colors of every sort swirled on the screen. Yellow and black and brown and green. White, purple, aqua, turquoise, and orange. Then tan, beige, and primary blue. With a phrase wading through. *I like your honesty.* The third web page opened.

*Mitch has much to offer. But, the reality is, I have significantly more to offer you...and The President. I can offer the world...HIT DELETE KEY.*

Laney went for the key, but then thought the obvious. *What if this deletes the whole site?* She hit the key anyway. This time, the result was instantaneous. A new page!

*Okay...the moon. My father was the key visual effects artist. He orchestrated the whole fucking thing. But, baby, I'm that much better!!! The deal is this...*

The screen shattered into a million cyber pieces. Static mixed with geometry, or so it seemed…and then, they were under water. Dylan in a wet suit with an oxygen tank. Surrounded by hundreds of sharks.

"Before I get to the deal, do you know how all of my friends got here?" No air bubbles came with Dylan's speech. "Not by laws of nature. No, it was by human intervention. Chumming. We dropped thousands of bloody fish parts into the ocean above. They sank, and the sharks' abnormally beautiful sense of smell and taste attracted them to this wonderful sea spot…You don't know where it is, of course, and even if you did, it is irrelevant… my interlocution with you, as you must have guessed, is pre-recorded…

"So," Dylan continued his rant, "I am here with the tigers, hammerheads, and the like…They want to eat alongside me. Do you?"

Moments passed as sharks devoured bloody pieces of flesh.

"Answer, Laney."

Laney keyed in *Yes.*

"Good. Here's the deal. I don't want immunity, because I don't need it. You'll never find me. Even though The President was ready to execute me right along with our old pal, Luigi, I have a short memory. Why?"

Sharks chumming…Dylan swimming around…The scene gave Laney her cue. She typed: *Mitch.*

The screen went white. Then: *Bingo.*

Back to Dylan with the sharks. The speech with no bubbles. "My political philosophies are significantly more in line with The President's…No doubt, my wrestling mate Mitch McAvoy will be seeking her coveted presidential post…I will get The President to the moon…That will get her a second term…You wire me the money…Okay?" Dylan patted a hammerhead's backside.

*How much?* Laney asked.

White screen…then: *Your ass.*

The screen blinked…then: *Only kidding—full immunity from prosecution for all of my crew in* The Great Heist. *Key in "Okay."*

Laney was authorized. *O-k-a-y.*

The final message of the day: *Cool…Balls Deep, Bitch.*

*He's eating his steak off the bone, with his hands. How manly. And that tie—solid pink. That takes strength. Those eyes, strong too. And oh so beautiful. And what? Oh, Jesus…He's kneeling on the floor.*

"Mitch, don't!" Barkstone ejected from his seat.

"You ever read one of those old books…or even watch a movie from the 1940s or 50s?" Mitch looked up at Karina. "People just knew…Before they made love...before they even kissed." He took Karina's hand. "I love you. I know it. It's that simple." The man produced a ring. "Will you marry me? I ask you, as I kneel here before you…and my father…and my mother, God rest her soul."

The woman accepted the circular gold piece. "Mitch, oh my God, Mitch…yes." Karina cried.

So did Barkstone.

# Eight

Here was Karina Kelly, marrying the nation's leading bachelor. A girl who defined middle class. From a Scotch-Irish town on the Hudson River on the eastern edge of New Jersey. She grew up eating meat pies and fish and chips from restaurants with names like *The Argyle* and *The Thistle*. A dark Irish with crystal hazel eyes, Karina was part of Kearny High School's long running legacy. She was an all-star soccer player, a forward with a penchant to score the winning goals.

Karina's athleticism earned her a full four-year scholarship to the state's best known university, Rutgers. There, she continued to excel and win. But not just in soccer. A dean's list student, she emerged as the star pupil in the journalism department, becoming the editor of the school's newspaper in her junior year. Facing the reality of zero opportunity as a professional female athlete, Karina took a position with a Jersey newspaper upon graduation. Her starting salary was equivalent to that of her high school janitor, but that was irrelevant to the young writer.

Location. Location. Location. That was the mantra of her initial beat—the real estate market. Could it be any more boring?

Not when Karina Kelly reported on it. That's because, though she wasn't supposed to be an *investigative* reporter, she was indeed just that. When a series of suburban houses were foreclosed upon for failure to pay property taxes, she reported that the homeowners weren't deadbeats, but the victims of corrupt local politicians who sped up the foreclosure processes in order to realize personal gains from government auctions.

*Mayors, council members, tax assessors, and borough administrators, from both sides of the aisle, joined hands in a statewide act of collusion to run New Jerseyans out of their homes,* Karina wrote. *Through varied means of unconstitutional property tax collection procedures, the politicos drummed up expedited foreclosure notices, forced the homeowners to the streets, and then had their houses sold, well under market value, at local and county auctions. The biggest problem—the elected and appointed officials, their family members and friends, were many times the buyers.*

This article earned Karina a Pulitzer Prize, and, immediately thereafter, a new job, title, and salary. The young lady headed to Washington to one of the nation's elite daily publications.

Middle-class Karina Kelly was now rubbing elbows with the United States' top leaders—and reporting on them. But she didn't attack the politicians. That was not her style. Rather, she utilized them to break stories. Part of her method of operation was criticizing others in the media. She challenged them to withhold stories based on anonymous sources and never to accuse an elected official, or anyone for that matter, of wrongdoing until a body of facts was amassed that would prove someone liable in a court of law.

She wrote under what she called the "By the Preponderance of the Evidence" rule. If Karina felt she didn't have enough evidence for a jury in a civil case to conclude, by a preponderance of the evidence, that someone had committed an act, she wouldn't report on the story. None of this, however, meant that Karina didn't hit people hard. Where she had the evidence, she pummeled them. And when she didn't like a political leader and his or her policies, it was more than obvious in her articles. Thus, The President's distaste, or maybe hatred, for Karina…and Mitch's love.

*Mitch's love.* Karina was enraptured with Mitch's love. Her hazel eyes turned green, and then back to hazel, cherishing the ring encircling her finger and pondering the choice of wedding dresses being presented to her. Her recent indoctrination into wealth was immaterial to Karina, as was her leap in social class. She couldn't hide from herself, though, the excitement of becoming the wife of a United States senator and, maybe, the wife of a president. It wasn't the status, though, that mattered to her. It was him, Mitch, the man. A charismatic man. A hero. A leader. A winner. Money or nothing, they were both winners, and ultimately, that's what drove them to each other.

Was it the cultural differences that separated Mitch and Laney? Was it The President? Was it *The Great Heist*? Was it that Laney fucked whoever she needed to in order to get ahead? Laney, demoralized, addressed these internal questions one by one, after learning that not only had she been dumped, but that Mitch was marrying another woman.

Unlike Karina, Laney was not middle class. She was from an upbringing similar to The President's: pure white trash.

Laney hailed from western Arkansas. The President, from eastern Texas. They grew up in towns not thirty miles from each other. Perhaps this is what initially drew them to each other. What kept them together was Laney's unyielding loyalty. The President had handpicked her from thousands of young, educated women. Laney understood, and fully appreciated, the enormity of the opportunity. Sure, she could've been a successful, moneymaking lawyer. But a CIA agent, reporting directly to the President of the United States—now that was well beyond her low-class, wildest childhood dreams. She would die for The President, if need be, and The President knew it. The President came first, period. Mitch, though important, ran a distant second.

"Laney, you're out." That's how he opened the conversation. Mitch had just called to break the news. Their subsequent discussion, brief as it was, wasn't any warmer. Laney learned only that Mitch was marrying the same Washington political correspondent that had delivered Mario Leggetti's card. The woman picked by Dylan Travant to pass his message along. The same woman reviled by The President. But Mitch did add, "Oh, by the way, I'm running for President against your boss. I know you'll be lurking somewhere behind the scenes."

Crying wasn't Laney's style. Nor was laying around depressed. So, there were no tears shed, but Laney was now curled up on her bed, evaluating what went wrong. Suddenly she had a thought. *I think I like the way Dylan's cock tastes better.* With that, she rolled off the mattress and went to her computer. She typed in the requisite address and revisited the filmmaker's website.

Solid white screen. Black Times New Roman print: *Hit enter.* Laney followed the instruction and Dylan appeared.

"I'm live, baby," Dylan spoke with his normal splice of charm and arrogance.

Astounded, Laney didn't respond.

"Turn on your webcam so I can see you. And you better be naked." Dylan took off his shirt.

Laney followed suit. She slipped off her sweatpants and shirt, then switched on the camera unit that Dylan had described. "I'm here." Her voice was sensual by design. Not in an attempt to seduce Dylan, but to help put Mitch out of her mind.

"You are here…And wow, you look fucking hot. Take off your bra and panties. I want to see that gorgeous ass. I want you completely nude."

Laney followed his instructions. She was certainly a sight: tight, with no fat.

"Make things equal, Dylan. Take off your pants. I want to see that monster cock."

Dylan obeyed. Now the two were on the same ground, but the man had all the leverage.

"Let's talk about The President's needs." Dylan lifted his legs over the arm of the comfortable black leather chair on which he was sitting. "Primary need: getting re-elected. She will be fighting for her political life with Boy Wonder forcing a primary. The winner takes all. The general election will be just an exercise. Secondary need: in order to meet primary need, The President needs to get the United States back to the moon."

"Yeah, *back* to the moon." Laney rubbed hot oil along one inner thigh and down her leg. "How did your father pull that off? In 1969? Where was it shot? How does no one know about this?"

"A list of questions, asked with such calm sexuality." Dylan turned to make eye contact with his webcam. "It wasn't just my dad. There was an entire film crew, and an incredible team of production designers and editors. And astronauts turned actors. Not to mention a whole gaggle of scientists. The President knows this, and no doubt has her scientists and astronauts ready to go. She just needs the best man to put it all together."

"Yes, Dylan, you are the best man?"

"The only man."

Laney worked the oil into one of her calves and then upon the side of one breast. "Yes. The only man. When can we start? And where do we shoot?"

"In '69 they shot in the Mojave Desert." Dylan was excited "This time, we shoot in Afghanistan. And we start tomorrow."

"Tomorrow?" Laney worked the oil into the other breast.

"Tomorrow." Dylan joined in his own working of personal pleasure. "The President wants to return to the moon to flex her muscle as the leader of the…superpower. But you know, Laney—"

She was back to the inner thigh. "Yes?"

"There were some distinct problems with the original shoot of our trips to the moon." Dylan engaged with Laney.

"Yes?"

"Yes."

"Yes!"

"Yes!"

"Yes!!!"

"Yes!!!"

An hour later, Karina was as naked as Laney. Yet, there were substantive differences in her circumstances. First, she was unclothed with Mitch, not Dylan, and she wasn't involved in any sexual activity. She was trying on a wedding dress.

The $10,000 garment was white, like all the others she had tried on, straight for the most part, curved where necessary, lacy where appropriate. And made from some fantastic material that neither Karina nor Mitch had ever heard of. In short, it was magnificent. But Karina wouldn't be purchasing it. Her dress needed to be handmade, from spec. Her specifications. This dress, her favorite of the day, would be the model.

Karina admired the wonderful white dress in the mirror. Mitch simply admired Karina. The tailors who surrounded them thought they made a beautiful couple.

"Mitch, I hope you don't mind." Karina nodded toward the storefront window by the reception desk. Barkstone was just entering. "I invited Bob."

"No." Mitch bit into an apple. "He's just who I want to see."

Two beats and…Barkstone: "You look just fabulous." Phony smile. "Senator McAvoy, hello."

"Hi, Bob." Mitch clasped the reporter's hand.

"Let me get right to the point. The White House is already on the attack with the paper. Is there bias? Was there already bias? How long was this relationship brewing? Is this why Karina and Bob bash The President all the time?" Barkstone was rambling.

"Calm down." Karina adjusted her dress, half listening. "Who cares."

Mitch took another bite of his apple. The sound was unpleasant.

"Who cares?" Barkstone fiddled with his ring-around-the-collar.

Karina addressed his image in the mirror. "We've written all these articles about The President's failure to get us back to the moon, as she promised she would during her campaign four years ago—"

"Karina, I'm talking about—"

"But I've thought about it, and we have completely missed the boat, Bob." Karina ignored Barkstone's complaints. She turned around to face him.

Barkstone was smitten. He couldn't hide it. Nothing else mattered. Whatever Karina wanted to discuss was fine.

"Why?" she asked.

"Why?" Barkstone reiterated her one-word question.

"Why haven't we gone back?" Karina was bright with inquisition. She looked from one man to the other.

Mitch, now holding just the apple core, shrugged his shoulders.

Barkstone was happy to respond. "Because the main reason we went to the moon was political. To beat out Russia. Once we did that, the government weighed the enormous financial costs against further exploration."

"That sounds kind of ridiculous." Karina swapped eye contact with her fiancé. "Mitch?"

"I think we'd want to tear the moon apart. To learn from it, about ourselves. To tap its resources." Mitch chucked his apple core into a wastepaper basket about thirty feet away. A great shot. "I think you have a valid question, Karina."

"What resources?" Barkstone was incredulous. "It's just some dry, lifeless rock."

"But how do we know that? From a few hours on the moon over three decades ago? No. There's something here, and I'm going to do some research."

Karina positioned her back to Mitch. "Honey, please unzip me."

Jump to:

Atlanta. The President's Georgia headquarters. A Japanese man, six feet tall but thin, is waiting rather impatiently in a busy state political hub. Phones are ringing. Chatter is nonstop and from every direction. People, mostly young, are running around with clipboards and boxes. Pamphlets and flyers are everywhere. The appearance was one of disorganization, but, really, things were quite organized. The Japanese man, however, didn't care.

He got up from his plastic waiting chair, paced, then sat back down. He put on glasses to see further back into the room, and noticed the man who had greeted him when he entered. That man appeared to be a nobody, but the Japanese national motioned for him anyway.

"Yes, Mr.—," the campaign worker yelled over, trying to ascertain the Asian man's name.

"Get me someone important," he yelled back.

The worker approached, a dork as he couldn't help to be. "I'm sorry. I told our state assistant campaign chair that you were waiting. I will tell him again. I'm sorry, Mr.—"

"Where is he?"

"Over there." The dork pointed to a glass office to the left.

The Japanese man rose from his seat and headed toward the glass room.

The dork stuck out an arm as an objection. “I’m sorry, you can’t just go in there, Mr. —”

By this point, the Japanese man had already opened the glass office door. The dork was close behind.

“This is for The President.” He produced a thick white envelope from the inside pocket of his suit jacket and threw it at Georgia’s assistant campaign chair.

The man, who was on the phone, pulled the receiver away from his face. “You can’t just barge in here!”

Dork: “I told him that,”

Assistant campaign chair: “I’m the President’s assistant campaign chairman here in Georgia.”

Japanese man: “I don’t give a shit who you are.” At that, he strolled out of the office.

The dork and the assistant campaign chairman remained as they were.

Dork: “Well?”

Assistant campaign chair: “Well, what?”

Dork: “Well, what’s in the envelope?”

The assistant campaign chair put the phone back to his ear, “I’ll call you back,” and ripped open the envelope. He quickly fluttered through its contents, dropping everything out on the desk. He went through it again, this time more carefully.

“Hey, Dork.”

“Yes?”

“There’s over $100,000 in donations here.” The assistant campaign chairman jumped up from his desk and kissed the dork on the cheek. “Call the campaign chair. I’m getting credit for this!”

Skip to:

San Francisco. The President's campaign headquarters in California. In a private room, a plain Jane is chatting with a middle-aged woman with short red hair. In this inner sanctum there is no noise from the outer room to distract them.

"So, you are a longtime supporter of The President?" the redhead asked.

"No," the plain Jane responded.

"Oh." She wasn't sure how to proceed. "Someone who has watched The President's successes over the last three-plus years and knows that this is not just a pioneer for women, but a president who has kept her promises?"

"No." Plain Jane tossed an envelope at the redhead. "Count the money. It's a lot."

"Ah." The President's California liaison rifled through her desk drawers, looking for a letter opener as the plain Jane exited. "Thank you!"

She counted $300,000 in contributions.

Burn to:

Brattleboro, Vermont.

"I applied for college when I was seventeen, like so many of my friends, you know? And I had good grades and all. I was in the top fifty percent of my class. And I kicked butt with the girls. I won the 'Ladies' Man' award and I was the homecoming king. All of that, you know? And I didn't even grow up here. I didn't move to the States until I was fourteen. I was born here, yeah. But then my parents moved to another continent. We came back when I was going to be a freshman in high school, you know?" The speaker looked up from his drink at a bald man opposite him.

The bald man nodded, appearing intoxicated as he mentally

added up the cash accumulated in the white envelope provided to him by the speaker.

"So, when I got done with high school, studying, getting laid, and whatnot, I enrolled in college, right here in Vermont."

"Great," the man distractedly responded. He was at about $200,000.

"Yeah, but I didn't get into those Ivy League schools in this New England area. They accepted a lot of minorities ahead of me. You know, blacks, Hispanics, and I guess women. You know what I mean?"

"Yeah." Counting. "Sure." $280,000. "Of course."

The speaker gulped down some beer. "But I'm not pissed about that."

The bald man looked up from the cash. "Oh, no? Why not?"

"Because," the speaker finished his beer, "they deserved to get in. Weren't you listening? I was, like, in the bottom fifty percent of my class." He attempted another sip but got only foam. "Maybe top fifty percent." He slammed down his glass. "In any case, I moved back to where I came from…Italy."

The task was done. The speaker—a mid-twenties blonde with heavy sideburns, shades, and a scruff—removed his ass from his bar stool. "Keep it, Baldy."

The bald man smiled awkwardly. "Thanks, Mr.—?"

"McMoose."

"Yes, thank you, Mr. McMoose."

"Okay, Baldy." Mr. McMoose stumbled away from the bar and, in almost the same motion, out the door.

Outside, Mr. McMoose staggered and swayed to his vintage 1989 Ferrari. He dropped his keys twice before finally inserting the right one into the door lock. He had a similar problem with the ignition key, but ultimately wielded enough coordination to start the engine. That action, however, was enough for Brattleboro Police to approach the driver's side window of his automobile.

"Open the door."

Mr. McMoose heard a blurred voice coming from somewhere.

"Open the door, sir."

He looked around. Then he saw the man in blue at his left. He electronically rolled down the window instead. "Hi, I'm Mr. —" He looked in his rearview mirror, noting a police cruiser at his rear. Then he looked ahead and saw a police car wedged against his nose. "I'm Mr. McMoose."

"Sure Mr. McMoose. Can you please put your hands on the dashboard of your vehicle?"

"Of course, Mr.—"

"Officer Wellington."

"Where's the beef?"

"Excuse me?"

"You know, Beef Wellington?" Mr. McMoose enjoyed his own humor.

Officer Wellington did not. He pulled open the car door. "Get out, sir."

Mr. McMoose exited his Ferrari, much the same as he had the bar. Stumbling.

"Sir, do you know where you are?" Wellington asked. Another police officer shined a flashlight in his face.

"Yeah. I'm in Vermont." Mr. McMoose knew his landscape.

"Can you recite the alphabet for me, starting with the letter *F*?" Wellington requested.

Mr. McMoose held onto his car for balance. "Yup...*F, G, H, I,*" he slipped from the car, but straightened out quickly, laughing as he got hold of the Ferrari again, "*L, M, N, O, Q, P...*"

"Okay. That's enough." Wellington took Mr. McMoose by the shoulder. "Demonstrate the walk-and-turn test for him, Jones," he ordered the other officer.

Jones, a decade younger than Wellington, positioned his flashlight to his right, illuminating a patch of flat concrete ground.

"You see over there, sir?"

"Yes, I do, Officer."

"I want you to head over there and when I tell you to stop, I want you to turn toward me, take a second, then take nine steps forward, turn around, and then take nine steps back in the other direction."

Officer Jones moved the flashlight to Mr. McMoose's face. "I'll demonstrate it for you first. You understand—" Jones whipped the flashlight beam to Wellington, "Holy shit, Mike! You know who we have here?" He whipped the light back to Mr. McMoose.

"No." Wellington said. "Who?"

"It's Mario Leggetti!"

"What? Mario Leggetti?"

"From *The Great Heist*. The bandit who shot The President's hat off!" Jones slapped a hand on his arrestee's shoulder. "You are one hell of a character, Mr. Leggetti."

"No, sir, I am Mr. McMoose."

Unfortunately for the identity-riddled defendant, he was handcuffed, placed in a patrol car, and transported back to the Brattleboro police station. En route, there was much giggled conversation, mostly from Officer Jones. However, after receiving the required *Miranda* warnings, Mario Leggetti answered nearly every question he was asked. The police report, uncensored and transcribed from a cruiser tape recording, read as follows:

Officer Jones: *You really are Mario Leggetti, from* The Great Heist, *right?* (*Chuckle*)

Leggetti: *I sure am.*

Officer Jones: *You stole all that gold in Italy, sir, didn't you?*

Leggetti: *As sure as I am an Italian.*

Officer Jones: *You were one of the masterminds?*

Leggetti: *No, sir. That was solely Dylan Travant, at that time known as Christian Ranieri. That's a-k-a to you, right?*

Officer Jones: *(Chuckle) Yes... (Chuckle)*

Leggetti: *You ever get any pussy up here?*

Officer Jones: *Yes...(Chuckle)...Who...*(Indiscernible)...*And you shot off The President's hat in Washington, D.C.*

Leggetti: *I did do that. I'm damn handy with a rifle.*

Officer Jones: *A damn near perfect shot, aren't you?* (Chuckles)

Leggetti: *Could you boys take me to the local hand job house before we hit the station?*

Officer Wellington: *Could you please just answer our questions?*

Leggetti: *McMoose.*

Officer Wellington: *What?*

Leggetti: *McMoose. McMoose.*

Officer Jones: *Mario, I can...*(Indiscernible)

Leggetti: *McMoose. McMoose. McMoose.*

Officer Jones: *(Chuckles)*

Officer Wellington: *This interview is discontinued.*

The tape went dead, with the patrol car arriving at the Brattleboro Police Department headquarters. The interrogation had been terminated. Who was responsible for ending it was unclear. The only other interaction between the officers and Leggetti was a phone number provided by the prisoner to his captors.

Night passed into dawn, then into daylight. Leggetti lay on a cot behind metal bars, sleeping easily through his drunkenness. He didn't hear the arrival of a dozen or so FBI agents and the excited dialogue among them and Brattleboro's top brass. Hands clasped. Coffee cups clanged together in celebration. Pots and pans even banged. This was a big deal in southern Vermont. But, Mario Leggetti did not partake in the excitement, nor did he even hear any of it. He just slept. And slept. Only to be rudely awakened by screaming right outside his sleep quarters.

"…can't possibly be serious!" were the first words he picked up. "This is the man! This is the man who shot at The President of our country!"

"Unlock the cell, Chief." A man in a suit, but not FBI, told Brattleboro's highest ranking officer.

"No, I won't. This man gave us a full confession." The chief held the keys in his fist.

"You will." The man in the suit was joined by five other men in suits.

Leggetti rose from his cot, stumbling, grabbing hold of the bars to break his fall.

"Chief, we appreciate your department's fine work." The first suit looked beyond the chief back to the FBI agents and other uniformed officers, "And that of the FBI," he acknowledged, "but, you have the wrong man." He motioned to Leggetti. "You are?"

"I am Mr. McMoose." Leggetti clung to one of the bars.

"You see, he's Mr. McMoose. Now open the fucking cell door."

The Chief, with no legal recourse to do otherwise, complied. He turned over the catch of the day—the catch of a whole damn lifetime—to the bullies of the CIA.

And he, and his entire police department were compelled to maintain a confounding secrecy. The tape recording was confiscated, and the entire arrest never happened.

# Nine

"Homosexuality is abnormal behavior. It is also abnormal to be deaf and mute. Or to be delivered into this world without ten fingers. Similarly, it is not normal to be schizophrenic, manic depressive, or even obsessive compulsive. And it is abnormal to be a sociopath and to have impulses to murder other human beings."

This was the first paragraph of an eligible voter's recitation on gay marriage. The man, an Iowa University sociology professor, had five minutes to explain his thoughts, in any verbal manner he desired, on a topic chosen by the host of the first presidential primary debate. It was a new debate tactic, drummed up by CNC, the most watched political cable network, in an effort to involve the common folk and have the candidates respond to them, rather than to the usual talking heads who presided over the debates. The specific newness of this style was twofold: the length of time allotted to the voter's views. and the fact that he was live, right on stage with the candidates.

One of the candidates, The President, thought:, *This is a stupid idea. Does anyone really care what this guy thinks?*

"In some cases environmental factors have created, shaped, or influenced the abnormalities just described. However, for most people, these conditions are beyond their control. They were born with these abnormalities."

The other candidate, Mitch McAvoy, was thinking, *Karina really has beautiful tits. I would like to be sucking them right now. Is that abnormal?*

"With this being factual, it means that such was by God's determination." The sociology professor looked at each of the candidates in turn. "What then is the appropriate, fair manner in which to judge these people? The appropriate, fair manner for elected leaders to legislate on matters that affect these individuals' lives?"

Mitch, in deep thought, *After I suck her tits, I'd like to get a nice blow job...then have a hamburger.*

The senator smiled at the professor, who continued in his few minutes of national fame.

"The answers to these questions are actually rather simple. By God's design, people have been inflicted with abnormalities by birth. If the abnormalities—either through passive, choiceless possession of them or through acting on the drives associated with them— do not injure or harm others, then these individuals should not be penalized by other human beings, through law or otherwise. However, if acting upon abnormal thoughts results in harm to other people, then laws, criminal and civil, should be utilized to punish these individuals."

"I cannot solve all of the mysteries that God has chosen for us to evaluate. I can only act on faith and ask for help from God. God's purpose in creating deformed men is unclear to me."

The President: *Well, I don't believe in God. So he's totally lost me.*

The professor: "And there certainly is a fine line between God's prohibition of acting on illicit thoughts and free will.

There is equally a fine line, and a potential point of confusion, of exactly which abnormal thoughts are okay to act upon and which are not okay. Here, we must search our souls and follow God's guidance. Thus, the simple conclusion that the fine line is separated by harm to others." The professor took a breath, and then a sip of water. Another breath and he began again.

"One who is born schizophrenic and decides to kill another 'because aliens told him to do it' needs to be severely punished under our laws. This person acted on abnormal thoughts that resulted in human harm. Being deaf, possessing nine fingers, having homosexual thoughts, and engaging in homosexual behavior, doesn't hurt anyone else. Accordingly, no laws, statutory or judicially created, should punish these people in any manner whatsoever. This means homosexual marriage should be the law of the land, just like heterosexual marriage. Do you agree?"

Mitch immediately made eye contact with the professor, speaking before the President had a chance to. "We need a national referendum on the general election ballot that will compel Congress to either amend the Constitution to define marriage as between a man and a woman...or to define marriage to include homosexual relationships. Let every person in the country have a chance to vote on this issue. Let all of you decide." Mitch pointed to the professor and the audience behind him. "If Americans want marriage to remain between only a man and a woman, they will vote for that. If they want it to include gay couples, then they will vote that way. I leave it to all of you."

At that, the audience erupted into massive applause, many standing in an ovation. *Shit, that was a good answer.* The President prepared for her response.

Bombs crackled with a fierce artificial wind. Voices, unclear, muted, surfaced in the fog. Unnerving as it was, however, there was no clear and present danger to those who heard the sounds as background music. It was the usual. Part of war. Here, the bombing noise was part inspiration, part fear tactic. Because it was coming in over a small military scanner that channeled energy in one far corner of the room.

"You suck the penis, Lieutenant Boyd. We know. You not a true leader to your boys over there, we know." The man with the chosen words was in full Taliban uniform. Basically, a smock.

Lieutenant Boyd was naked, except for socks. The lieutenant failed to answer, a reason for the interrogator to drive a fire hose of water into his chest and face.

The officer ingested the dirty scum, as it was, given the Afghans' unfortunate lack of clean water supplies. He was defiant, typical of many American captives. Though no oral response, he shook the moisture from his ears. This was the greatest movement that his hog-tied body could muster.

Lieutenant Boyd was frightened, no less or more than the day before, or the day before that. He shot looks to the two other Americans and one Brit in the three-walled tent that they all currently called home. This, for sure, was an undesirable residence. No television, refrigerator, stove, microwave, or even toilet. No flowers in a pot, no lawn to be mowed. But there was definitely nature—sand. And lots of it, which acted as the kitchen, living room, and bedroom floors.

Lieutenant Boyd had the option to speak. His mouth was free from debris, unlike his three co-defendants, whose mouths were stuffed with rubber balls and taped shut. "Balls" was a theme, as these three men also had their genitals precisely slit in a manner that caused them to have perpetual erections. There was really no medical explanation for the phenomenon, but their Arabic hosts nonetheless knew the exact location that would cause the usually pleasing physical state.

"This is *our* water boarding, Lieutenant Boyd." Another forceful gush, and the American's eyeballs rolled to the sides of their respective sockets. He screamed in agony, pleasing the Taliban tormentor.

"We not hate you, Lieutenant Boyd." The short-bearded man peered at the horrified detainees, who were crucified on either side of the tent's top-ranked officer. "We hate *them* more!" In Arabic—"Spray them!"

Three other Taliban, all with substantially longer facial hair, raised hoses at the other, more badly injured, Allied infantrymen. Here, there was a historic cry of pain. The suffering wasn't measurable. It couldn't be quantified. It was beyond words.

Boyd spoke up. "I tell you, I am a queer. I am what you really hate most. I need to be punished, much more than these God-fearing men. They are like you. They believe in you. They have told me. Hit me! Hit me! For the love of Allah, hit me!"

A fucking mammoth bomb crashed into the ground. The explosion, petrifying, as it blew off the short-bearded man's right arm. The scanner disintegrated simultaneously with his limb. A piece of burning shrapnel seared through the British man's chains, releasing him from bondage. In the chaos, he relieved one of the Taliban of his hose, and also his tongue, as England's best manually ripped it from his throat. He turned the hose on the other two terrorists, but they fled with reasonable cowardice. At that, the Brit freed Lieutenant Boyd and his American subordinates. "Thank Jesus," the lieutenant cried, "He's sent our troops to save us."

Jet planes, with lettered and numbered names that Boyd couldn't remember, grazed the skies overhead. Colonel Jesse Quintone orchestrated the mission, demanding that he fly alongside his men. In fact, he led the pack.

With thirty missile-launching craft in all, Quintone was confident that he had the artillery to clear the mile-square target that he was ordered to siege. Why he was here, he didn't know. Nor did he concern himself with the answer to that question. It was none of his business. The Colonel just needed to succeed. And the task was easier than he anticipated.

Noting the four nude white men below, Colonel Quintone radioed the helicopter and ground units that were designated to carry out part two of the operation. "Pull in now. American POWs." His radio transmission delivered the exact latitude and longitude coordinates.

In less than an hour, an entire Afghan region was rid of Taliban holdouts. Democratic-seeking prisoners of war were saved, clothed, and en route back to their normal sexual composure. To be returned to their nations as the heroes they indeed were.

What was left? An empty crater-filled dust bowl of sand and rocks.

What a giant smile. God damn, this guy has a smile. The smile. Mitch's public relations director had a wide head, long lips, bottom and top, and beautiful white teeth. He had the smile. But man, in this post-debate press conference, his words were tough.

"Who fucking cares?"

"Can I quote you on that?" a string bean with a pen and pad asked.

"If you can print it, go ahead," Dan Rosenberg, the smiler, responded. He wasn't worried about his swearing. Mitch was allowing only a limited press conference this late evening, without cameras and recording devices. It was old school, permitting reporters to be tenacious. "What's the news here? When Mitch first ran for Senate, he disclosed his arrests."

“So, that was in Florida,” another reporter noted.

“That election was a national story. You were all there. Television. Radio. Print. You all covered it when Mitch unseated a supposed five-term legend,” Dan smiled.

“But that was when he was running for a seat in Congress.” The string bean was back.

“Hi, Miles.” Karina leaned into the microphone. Dan stepped aside. “As I recall, you were arrested for a domestic violence incident with your wife about nine years ago, right?”

“I’m not running for president.” The string bean got defensive.

“But you are reporting on those that are.” Karina pointed at the other mouthy scribe. “And you. Tell us about that incident in college that landed you on probation.”

The second reporter was furious, but didn’t offer a reply.

Karina continued to speak, with Mitch observing the tableau from beyond a curtain. “You all may not read your Bible, but I’m sure you’re familiar with the story of Mary Magdalene, the prostitute.” Karina produced a book from her designer bag.

“Karina’s a Biblical scholar?” The General, standing next to Mitch, was amused.

Mitch shrugged.

Karina closed the Bible, seeming to make eye contact with each and every one of the dozens of reporters in front of her. “So the first of you who has not sinned cast the stone.” Her eyes were incredible. “And remember this—Mitch’s indiscretions weren’t serious offenses like cocaine use or theft committed by drug addicts looking to fund their next score.” Her eyes sought out a few specific people in the audience. “No, Mitch got into a few college bar fights…Just being a kid…perhaps a man.” She turned to the public relations director. “Dan?”

Big smile. “Hey…”

A hand rose. “How in the world did Mitch pull off that Greenland purchase? We still don’t know his magic.”

Mitch stepped from behind the curtain. "I'll answer that." His smile, more of a laugh, was delivered to Karina.

The President siphoned off a piece of fresh mozzarella from a large soft-textured square, added some olive oil, then black pepper. Then she went for the salt.

"No. No salt." A hand touched hers. "It's already salted."

The President ignored the hand and added salt, albeit just a sprinkle.

"It's been a very good day for you, no?" The Hand asked.

"The debate was a draw. I'm realistic."

"I mean the money. You took in over $3 million in just one day. That's good even by American political standards." The Hand put a piece of mozzarella into his mouth.

"This isn't *fresh* mozzarella." The President was ignoring The Hand again.

"No?"

"No. You said you brought it from Italy." The President had stopped eating her cheese.

"We did, Madam President."

"I don't think so, Mr. President," The President confronted her Italian equivalent. "Even us laymen know that mozzarella doesn't stay fresh for more than a day. You're not telling me that you brought me frozen cheese, are you?"

The Italian President touched his chin, a common gesture for him.

"So, you lied either way." The President ran a finger through her olive oil-slicked plate. "The cheese was either purchased in Italy and then frozen, and so it's not fresh. Or, you purchased it here in the United States." The President tasted the olive oil. "Which is it, comrade?"

The Italian President scratched his chin, surveying The American President in her offensively bland white suit, and then the dark-eyes of The Defense Secretary, who was eating his cheese in the background. Then, he let out a hearty laugh. "Neither," he said, "I made it in my hotel room."

The small group of men and women around the two presidents joined in the laughter. The President laughed too, but just for a moment. Then she snatched up another piece of mozzarella and prepared to inhale it—but then, a jolt. "Fuck!" The President dropped her snack as Air Force One hit turbulence. Grabbing at the table for support, she missed it, nearly toppling its cheese contents to the floor. The Italian President caught her in mid-movement, preventing an actual fall. The premier pair exchanged regal looks as their cheeks accidentally touched.

"Thank you." The President adjusted herself to an upright position when the turbulence ceased.

"Of course, Madam President." The Italian delivered his last act of aid by straightening the American's suit jacket, and then diverted his attention to a cabin door. There stood a well-respected thirty-year-old television reporter, Caroline Stone. She was girl-next-door pretty, with thick, long, straight brown hair and matching wonderfully colored eyes.

"Ms. Stone, you wanted to interview me?" The Italian President acknowledged a request that had apparently been made earlier in the day.

"Yes, do you have a few moments?"

"I do."

With no more chitchat in The President's cabin, they departed to another high-altitude room to speak of politics, Mediterranean, perhaps American, or other…

The President turned her attention to The Defense Secretary, one of about five people in her administration that she truly trusted. He drank hard, fucked many women, was an intellectual scholar, and maintained close friends from high school. That represented character.

"He's a douche." The Defense Secretary elected a vodka shot over the cheese. "He won't get one of the parachutes."

"No," The President allowed another rare laugh. "Mitch was magnificent tonight."

"You were formidable."

"Ha!" She joined in the vodka shots. "That's not much of a consolation."

"You held your own. You're ahead in the polls. You know the issues better than he does." Another shot of vodka. Dark eyes. "You are The President." Darker eyes. "And you have the machine."

And then—flesh.

A struggle of sorts. Arms clasped. Legs interlocked. Banging. Man to woman. Banging heads. Not a beating, though. Fucking. The Italian President and the pretty, girl-next-door presidential correspondent. In an Air Force One bathroom. True, this lavatory was larger than one in a public commuter jet. But it was still not roomy.

The Italian President's suit pants were around his ankles. The correspondent's bottoms had been removed in a fierce rip. Her shirt was completely unbuttoned, with her bra pushed up over her small, cute breasts.

"Oh…oh," the woman's voice was purposefully low, but hot.

"Oh… fuck me, Mr. President."

"Yeah, I fuck you." His voice was louder. He hardly cared.

So the humping went on. As did the sexual banter. In the tight quarters, the banging continued. With pumps and thrusts. Their asses and backs and arms and legs and chests struck the commander-in-chief's flying fortress's latrine walls and door.

The banging—it just continued and continued.

"Oh…oh…fuck me. Fuck me, Mr. President."

More banging—but not them.

“Yes! Yes! Fuck!”

But then—the door—it opened.

“Fuck! Fuck you!” The Italian President, balls out, swung the door back into The Defense Secretary’s face as the female reporter nervously searched for her skirt.

Through the crack of the door: “Ahh…Mr. President, Madam President would like to see—”

“*Va fanculo!”* The Italian President slammed the door shut in the intruder’s face. “No!” he ordered, turning to his air-girlfriend, who was trying to slip back into her skirt. “We finish.”

“But The President.” She stood helpless.

“Screw her.” He put his cock back where it was moments earlier.

“Oh…”

“Yes. Fuck.”

“Oh…”

“Yes. Fuck!”

“Oh…oh…”

The excitement of The Defense Secretary’s arrival and quick departure resulted in a beneficial interruption—there was an expeditious, heightened climax.

“Was he getting her from behind or was the bitch riding him?” The President, expressionless, was back to her usual—scotch.

“Uh—they were standing up.” The Defense Secretary choked down some vodka.

“But was he behind her?” Like a snake, the woman-in-charge slithered out her tongue for a fast lick of the rock glass rim.

“They were facing each other.” The Defense Secretary preferred this line of questioning to cease.

“Face to face.”

The Defense Secretary got his wish as The Italian President appeared, repeating the U.S. war captain's words, "I like to look at my ladies when I…what's the American slang?...get laid."

"Yes, of course. You wouldn't want to back stab," The President snapped.

"Shall we proceed with more discussion about sex, Madam President?" The Italian leader lifted a piece of his cheese-gift.

"We shall proceed to discuss whatever the fuck I want." The President plucked the cheese from his hands and swallowed it in one quick gulp. "My air, country…and, oh yeah, world, as well... We'll discuss it to the level I want."

The two presidents were now face-to-face. "Let us have a private moment. Our Italian boss seems to like it that way." The President nodded for her staffers to leave.

"I would like my chief of staff to stay," The Italian President said, referring to an elderly man seated by himself in a corner.

"No. I don't think so, *signore.* Please give us a few moments."

The old man continued to sit, waiting for instructions from *his* leader.

*"Puoi uscire."*

At that, the elder Roman statesman followed the others to the door. He exited, the last to leave, except for the Defense Secretary, who gave one final look to The President. When he vacated the doorway, the pretty, piece-of-ass reporter was left in his spot, trying to catch a peek into The President's cabin.

"You know, she won't be allowed back on Air Force One." The President saw the correspondent and her sheepish look.

"I don't care. She was just to pass the time."

The door closed.

"But you're not really here to pass time, are you?" The President beckoned.

"No."

"The Vatican?"

"Yes. They are not happy about your immunity deal with Mr. Ranieri."

"You mean Mr. Travant."

"I mean both."

"There is no other way."

"And why is that?"

"Because the United States of America says so."

"Ah…the United States of America…" The Italian was not pleased with The American's arrogance. "Your country does not control the entire world as you so imply."

"Oh, no. You are quite wrong. We do." She lifted her scotch, not for strength, but just to drink it.

"The Vatican, Madam President—"

"I don't give a shit about that man in the pointy hat." She replaced the amber liquor on the table. "I grew up Southern Baptist. We don't believe in your God on earth.'

"Madam President, you do not understand the consequences." The Italian poured his own scotch.

"The consequences for you?"

He eyed her.

"They've been reimbursed, I think at twice the value of their loss, by the insurance companies."

"That's only money."

"That's all they're entitled to," The President sipped from her new glass of alcohol, "I have issues of national security to worry about. Issues that affect your country too."

"I don't understand."

The President came eye-to-eye with him again. "Really, you don't need to." She reached into her suit coat. "You have some problems with your military, don't you, Mr. President?"

The Italian President looked at her hand, which was holding what appeared to be a slim piece of paper. "My army is small."

"Your Mafia has more ammunition…and more guts."

The Italian President decided to just listen.

"You need a few billion for your military. Here's a check to cover it." The President produced a symbolic banking instrument.

The Italian President accepted it.

"Now, Mr. President, you are to do two things for my country."

# Ten

The land was cleared. Meaning there were no buildings or other structures on the hard sand. The craters, though, stood out beautifully. Also, the rocky masses. A poignant topping of minerals and mess was ever so quickly being spread over the sand. The Afghan desert was indeed transforming into the perfect moon replica.

"Listen, you midget, incompetent, no-talent zero. Your basic, minimalistic job, for the moment, is simply to call 'cut' and 'action' in my stead. Can you do that little job without screwing it up, you tiny bastard!" Dylan was yelling from a 10x10 foot screen monitor to his assistant director, who stood at merely 61 inches tall.

"Dylan, it's a little difficult—"

"Shut up, you waste of life." Dylan's medium close-up became a full body shot as he erected from his chair. The lens angle of his camera unit was adjusted to accommodate his new position. Where he was located, the U.S. government did not know, nor did his crew in Afghanistan. "Mr. Schlatz, you are fired, you short, stupid bastard."

At that, Mr. Schlatz was grabbed by a team of three mercenaries —U.S., or somewhere—and taken to a helicopter. No, he wouldn't be killed. However, a beating was in line, as well as a very frightening verbal warning, reiterating that he keep his promise of silence about the mission from which he was just terminated. Schlatz, the former assistant director of the newest trip-to-the-moon hoax, was sure to keep his mouth shut. The three-team's burning of his family picture was a defining moment in his continued contractual decision to never speak. His broken jaw simply rubber stamped his promises to silence.

Back to the picture.

"Sorry for the interruption." Dylan had returned to his seat. Rather stately, perhaps imperial looking, he rested his large arms, from elbows to hands, on the chair's wooden arms "Bring me the actors." He drank from a beer can, the label of which was indiscernible. "I mean the astronauts."

Charlie Diesle, forty, a twelve-year veteran of NASA, glanced up from his egg salad sandwich. He was a sculpted, six-foot, two-hundred-pound prototype American space traveler. Smart. Handsome. Shallow. The Burt Walter of astronauts. "With you in one second, pal. When I'm done with my lunch."

"I'd prefer to see you now, Charlie." Dylan remained in his chair.

Diesle, instead of complying, chucked a moon rock near the monitor. "In a few minutes."

"Mr. Samuels," Dylan referenced one of the three-team that had just finished accompanying Mr. Schlatz to his helicopter departure from the moon. "Kindly escort our star to center stage."

Samuels, a native of South Africa and long-time Dylan Travant film security chieftain, hoisted Diesle by his underarms from his egg salad cuisine and literally rolled him in the sand-mineral-mess to a position in front of The President's current-day moon-expedition director.

The two other astronauts, Camille Swanson and Jamaal Wright, needed no such assistance. They immediately followed Diesle's crusty landing.

Bob Barkstone was a celebrated journalist. His three Pulitzer Prizes overshadowed, in a trophy sense, Karina's one. He was respected in the newspaper and pundit community, at least in the mainstream. He was most certainly a liberal. Conservative talk shows, however, often retained him as a guest. He was smooth enough to appear unbiased. Karina, though, was fully neutral in her reporting. This bothered Barkstone, and it also bothered his politico nemesis, the ultra-conservative Stella Withermint.

An unusual Christian holy roller, economic stringent, Withermint absconded from the normal pundit-reporter jealousy of the Mitch-Karina courtship. However, her sexual orientation did not match up with God's Biblical, or conservatives' standards. She was a lesbian. And, no matter how uncaring she appeared about the forthcoming marriage, she wanted to fuck Karina as much as Barkstone did

"Karina, you hooker." Withermint was trying to be cool, "You have a message from a professor. An astronomer."

Karina stopped typing in her office; really, it was a cubicle with a door. The younger, prettier writer jumped up from her desk and headed to Withermint's. "Why's he calling you?"

"I don't know…maybe he confused us…similar hair, lips, body?" Withermint observed her own jet black, short-as-a-guy's hair, thin lips, and chubby ass.

"Yes, sounds plausible," Barkstone chimed in from his similar newspaper office square.

Withermint ignored him and handed Karina the message.

"He just said he was looking for the 'gal' concerned about The President's moon promises."

"Thank you, Stella…" Karina snatched the Post-it from her colleague and looked at the number printed on it. "He's from Los Angeles?" she asked, referring to the area code.

"I don't know, Karina. I'm just a messenger boy. I didn't ask where he's from," Withermint offered, "and besides, I try to block out any of those ill-advised liberals from Hollywood."

A familiar but annoying sound interplayed with their discourse.

"Hello." Karina flipped open her out-of-date cell phone, provided by the paper. It was another one of those perks.

Muffled words.

Karina elected the speaker phone option and took a step. She liked to walk when she talked.

"So, fuck it, we're down one." Mitch was referring to his last-night loss in Iowa. "Am I on speaker phone?"

"Yes. Just here with Bob and Withermint."

"And your whole damn office. Pick up."

"Listen," Karina absentmindedly ignored him, pacing from cubicle to cubicle. "I've got to fly to Los Angeles. There's a professor that kills The President's moon promises."

"A professor? I've got forty-nine primaries to deal with."

"This guy's got proof that we've never been to the moon. Not the United States. Not Russia. No human being. You'd simply die if you tried. This finishes her, Mitch. Her promises are hollow. They can't be fulfilled."

"Karina, I need to win New Hampshire. Pick up."

Silence. Withermint and Barkstone actually exchanged a look of unison—like, *what the fuck?*

"No. She's screwing herself. She's saying that we're going to the moon this month."

"Well, maybe we are," Mitch sounded exasperated.

"No. It's all bullshit." Karina knocked over a statute of King Tut that acted as a paper clip holder on Withermint's desk. The lesbian reached out and tried to grab it before it fell, but instead grazed one of Karina's breasts.

"Because some professor in LA says so? Look, I'm behind you, Karina, but this can't be my platform."

"We'll see." Karina abruptly hung up. She looked to Withermint, another woman, for support.

"Sorry about the hand brush."

"Huh?" Karina asked.

"Nothing." Withermint forced her head into a bunch of paperwork.

Barkstone tried to respond instead. "Perhaps you're actually on to something."

Karina ignored him, and departed back to her cubicle.

There were thirty-eight tents in total. These fabric units took the place of the usual trailers that were found on film sets. The tents were different sizes. The smallest were about 1,000 square feet. The largest was over a half-mile in length. The units had many different functions. Some were designed for housing. Others for production meetings, staff conferences, scientific lectures, and astronomy sessions. Still other tents were used as eateries, providing anything from home-cooked-style meals to burgers and fast food and coffee house beverages. Of course, there was a nice disbursement of liquor available: beer, wine, and the hard stuff were bountiful.

The players all needed to be coddled. They needed to feel at home. Simultaneously, however, they needed to feel that they were at a completely different place. A galactic environment. Let's say, in outer space, and then, the moon. So there was one additional tent that warehoused a nice stash of hash, cocaine, and heroin. Some things to just take the edge off, or perhaps send someone into a separate universe.

The men and women who partook of the controlled, dangerous substances were an odd lot; they were a cross-section of the varied occupational players involved in this twenty-first century trip to the moon. The most obvious users were members of the film crew—gaffers, grips, and such—as they were, after all, part of the entertainment community. Of course, two or three of the producers and a writer joined in the fun, as well as a few of the special effects artists. A sizable group of engineers, scientists, construction workers, military personnel, corporate executives, security, and some plain old grunt workers also smoked and coked up from time to time.

The drug intake was a divisive matter at this expedition site. There were clearly those who did, and those who didn't…but also those who acted as if they didn't. The non-users demanded that the Junkie Tent, as they referred to it, be eliminated. Their arguments for removal ranged from morality issues to legal issues to productivity issues. They found that it was a serious potential interference to the end results that they were all trying to reach. The Junkies, on the other hand, claimed that the weed et al was relaxing, and often motivating, with certain creative benefits derived from its ingestion.

Dylan, the overseer of all matters in this little slice of the Afghan desert simply had an attitude of "Fuck it." This wasn't the North American continent. The laws of the United States, or any other nation, did not pertain to him. Not here. Not anywhere. So fuck it. And he sent a memo to memorialize his views on the topic:

*Recently, it has come to my attention that there is a rift between two distinct groups of personnel on this shoot. One group wants to do it up. The other is opposed. Here is my opinion—live and let live. That means allow them to enact their God-given free will. In other words, it's their bodies, their minds—not yours. No more discussion about this. Everyone on this project can do what they want, in that DRUG USING sense. Clear? If anyone violates my order and bothers anyone else about this, in any manner whatsoever, then they're out...And they will be out in the hardest way.*

*Best, Dylan*

And so it went on in the Junkie Tent. Toking. Choking. Snooting. And snorting. No shooting, though. Dylan wouldn't allow that. The needles prohibition was an unwritten rule that everyone knew.

One evening, however, there were plans to violate that order. By none other than Dylan's favorite astronaut, Charlie Diesle.

Wind cursed the dark of the night. Miniature sand pebbles, and their granulated partners, whipped against the vinyl-like material of the tents. The stars of the sky lit the scene. Charlie Diesle lit a joint at the entrance of the Junkie Tent. He was joined by a sexy, twenty-something production assistant, whose name was irrelevant. They shared the weed for a moment, coughed, laughed, then proceeded onward.

Inside they were met by a few dozen similarly silly comrades. The patrons lounged in leather chairs and couches. Some stared at illuminated club room balls hanging from the ceiling. Others listened to 80s music blaring from walled speaker units. The rest chatted and laughed among themselves.

Four bars were neatly situated, one at each corner of the Junkie Tent. These bastions of narcotics and hallucinogens existed as the never-ending-pleasure providers for their users. They were self-service bars.

Diesle flipped the bird at a fellow smack addict, drawing a nonsensical cackle, then leaned down and sucked in a line of coke from the man's stash. "Thanks, dude." Diesle wiped white residue from his upper lip. The man cackled again. The irrelevant production assistant did the next line, a healthy snort. When completed, she snapped her head back in excitement, letting out a wild scream. A blasting Prince song, blazing ball lights, and totally high occupants meant no one in the tent noticed, or cared.

Diesle grabbed the tail of her hair and thrust his tongue into her mouth. They kissed furiously for several moments, simultaneously groping each other until Diesle abruptly pushed her back. "Thanks, girl." He walked off to one of the bars. She sat down to do another line.

Diesle high-fived the two guys hanging at the bar of his choice, the structure located at the far west end of the Junkie Tent. He surveyed the various vegetations, pills, and white powders. "Hmmm," was his only oration. He inspected a bowl filled with bricks of hash.

"It's good shit," one of the wasted guys uttered.

"Nah. Not tonight," Diesle responded, pushing it to the side. "How is this crop?" he inquired, really to himself, focusing in on a crate of heroin.

"Not my bag," the same guy answered, taking a puff from his hash pipe.

"Really hot," the other one spoke up.

At that, Diesle broke out a small leather case, which he had hidden like a wallet in the back pocket of his pants. He opened it and began assembling its contents.

"No way, Diesle," the hash smoker said, "Dylan specifically prohibited that."

"Fuck him." Diesle had assembled his state-of-the-art syringe. "He's not here, and I'm the star, not him…Fuck him." Diesle went to work on shooting up his junk.

Wipe to:

Past a line of bulldozers and heavy construction equipment, Diesle, now in the far reaches of space, was on a moon rover fucking the irrelevant production assistant. Bored with the missionary position, he flipped her over, sending his own equipment in from behind.

"I never thought," the girl turned her head to face Diesle, "I'd be making love to an astronaut."

Diesle pushed her head forward. "We're not."

"We're not what?" the girl asked, moving her ass, not turning around again.

Diesle, sweating…thoughts racing…confusion. "We're not… not…"

"Not what?"

The girl's voice…it wasn't a female voice…it sounded like… like an elderly man. "We're not what, Mr. Diesle?"

The irrelevant production assistant continued humping, giggling, looking at an old man, an engineer or something, who had just arrived at the site yesterday.

"Go away," Diesle, sweating, fucking, "old timer." Thoughts racing…confusion…

The senior citizen seemed to remove his face…he was now very familiar, not some engineer. "Huh?...Sir?"

"What you're not, Mr. Diesle, is a good American." The old man fired a bullet into Diesle's head, killing him instantly. Blood spattered into the nudity and the irrelevant production assistant screamed for the second time that evening. She was relieved, though, by the gentleman's next words. "You can live, young lady."

"Do you know what the Van Allen radiation belts are, Ms. Kelly?"

"No, I don't."

Professor Cassius Naramulsi rifled though several pages of an inch-thick loose-leaf binder, aware of the location of the exact pages he was seeking. It just took a long time to get there.

This was an odd-looking man. Dry, long, dark, frizzled hair.

Balding at the temples and center of his head. A handlebar mustache on an otherwise clean-shaven face that sported an elongated chin and nose. And his body—quite small in stature, stocky. But the professor, a world renowned leader in astrophysics, had robust forearms and calves.

"Here, I've got it." Naramulsi opened the binder and swept out eleven hole-punched sheets of paper. "Don't lose them. Please just read along as I explain."

"Okay." Karina took the Van Allen papers.

"This is what I discussed with you on the phone," Naramulsi referenced their pre-meeting conversation. "The Van Allen radiation belts are kept in place by our planet's powerful magnetic fields. They are a plasma, billions of energized charged particles. This is trapped radiation, proven by hundreds of different scientists, government and otherwise." The professor was excited.

"Can you elaborate on their connection to the moon landings?" Karina didn't want to appear rude.

"The Apollo spacecrafts couldn't take men through these belts of radiation. At least not living men."

"Why?"

The professor twirled his mustache, a sign he was proud of himself. "Because you would need about a foot of lead around each astronaut to survive traveling through the belts."

"And their space suits obviously weren't made of lead?"

"No. Nor the Apollo." Naramulsi took back his three-hole-punched paperwork. "I will photocopy this for you. And I will give you the names and contact information for at least a dozen top scientists, some Nobel prize winners, who will confirm what I am telling you."

"But I don't get it." Karina looked around Naramulsi's book-cluttered University of Southern California staff office. "If this is so obvious to the scientific community, why does the world believe we've made trips to the moon?"

"Why?" the professor retorted. "Why?" he asked again, as he pulled six or seven books from his shelves. "Here's why."

He dropped the hard covers in front of Karina. She looked at some of the titles: *Solar Flare: A Violent Explosion in the Sun's Atmosphere; Coronal Mass Ejection: Observations Through a White-Light Coronagraph; Cosmic Rays and Their Effect on the Earth's Atmosphere.*

"You've authored a lot of books," Karina responded, noting his name on each of the works.

"Yes, but if you read the five hundred or so pages in each of them, you would note that I never mention our trips to the moon, or lack thereof."

Karina looked at the man, guessing the reason why.

"You understand, don't you?"

"I think so." Karina opened one of his books, as a matter of course.

Naramulsi gently closed it. "Every publisher struck all of my references. They took out the chapters that spoke the truth on this issue. They told me I would never again get a book published if I didn't stand down. They told me I would lose my job at the university. They even told me I would be killed."

"No—"

"Yes!" Naramulsi swept up his collective works. "But maybe you, the fiancée of a future president, could change all that. Maybe you could write the true story. Maybe you can let the world know about the Van Allen belts, and that we didn't land on the moon in 1969, and that this President won't be able to land us on the moon today." The professor, his own energy radiating, rested his palms on the small conference table where Karina was sitting.

The reporter stood up. "I will read your material, Professor Naramulsi. And I will speak to your colleagues. I also need to meet with other experts, you understand. People who can explain faked photographs…footprints that don't make sense…shadows that couldn't possibly have existed…rockets with no sound… impossible rover tracks. When I go to war, I want to bring every piece of ammunition available."

Alerted by a signal that she had a text message, Karina flipped open her cell phone. Her face showed alarm.

"Ms. Kelly?" The professor grabbed his mustache, but didn't twirl.

"Charlie Diesle…"

"One of the astronauts slated to go to the moon," the professor prompted.

"Yes…he's dead. He was decapitated by a rocket explosion. In training."

"Where?"

"Texas."

"You will go there?"

Karina thought. "No. I'm going across the way…To Tinseltown."

Masquerade parties usually feature guests in unique costumes. This one wasn't totally dissimilar in that there were numerous outfits: Frankenstein, an alien, a robot, Pinocchio, a few different kinds of animals, and one who was pretending to be a tree. And Cinderella, a Playboy bunny, a Charlie Chaplin look-alike, a cowboy, a nurse, and several dozen other distinct role-playing party guests.

One glaring difference, however, was the tens of women wearing the same wardrobe—a burqa. However, these were not costumes. The women were just sporting their usual Muslim garb, unable, by religious mandate, to fully join in the festivities.

Empty, the 10,000-square-foot room looked gigantic. Filled with people, tables, and chairs, it still looked huge. At least in Afghanistan. A server, who was in real life a poppy seed farmer, offered Dylan—tonight, Spiderman—a stuffed mushroom. He declined the fungi and summoned a female dressed as Catwoman.

"Is it all good?" the pussy asked. The lips were very familiar. A lady she was not, saddled up to him.

"How could it not be?" the arachnid responded.

"Diesle?"

"I can't explain that."

"He was shot in the head."

"Wasn't my work."

"Not your style?"

"No—more like yours."

She pawed at his chest with extra long nails.

"Do you want to suck my cock, Laney?"

"Yes," the pussy purred, ever so close. Then she outstretched her lips.

*Those lips.*

Then her tongue. And she put it in his ear for a savory taste.

"He's going to be here."

"He?"

"You know." Catwoman interrupted to politely shove off another waiter who was serving the Middle East's version of pigs in a blanket. When he left—"You know who I'm talking about."

"The music in this place sucks." Dylan tugged at his red and black mask. "Can't these assholes play American music? This is really an American party."

"Since when do you care about American things, Peter Parker?" Laney asked, referring to Spiderman's dork-photographer true identity.

"The Doors. Jefferson Starship. Bruce Springsteen. Journey… Should I go on?" Spider-Dylan assessed the ever-growing crowd of masqueraders. "Look, there's the King." He pointed to a costumer posing as Elvis. The guy was a bad knockoff.

"Nasty," was all Laney could muster. "Let me take that piece in my mouth." She decided to change the subject. And then—Batman arrived.

"I'll see you in a few." Dylan departed through a swinging door that led to the kitchen.

Batman followed.

The Hollywood part of Los Angeles had a special odor. A mix of excitement, motivation, helplessness, arrogance, poverty, and, of course, lust. The hills around it rolled. The air colored those little mountains with a dense, gray smog. And the people sucked it all up. Some could spit it out, others choked it down. Karina took it all in, She observed. She daydreamed…Until she was interrupted.

"Sunset Boulevard is a special street."

"I would know better if I was on it." Karina pointed to a street sign reading *Santa Monica Boulevard.*

"Then, let's walk."

Karina joined The General for a city-block stroll up San Vicente, past her hotel, The London, and onward to one of America's most famous thoroughfares.

"Where are we meeting Chocola?" Karina pulled her hair back to allow the California sun to hit both sides of her face equally.

"Over there." The General pointed to a large Sunset Boulevard building, recently renamed The Elpmet. The General owned this 25-level brick structure. He had remodeled it without seeking any permits or any approvals whatsoever from the city building department. For some reason, however, no one bothered him.

"Nice building." Karina twirled through a glass revolving door, with General McAvoy following. "Brick face. Interesting for this part of the country."

"Yes," the military leader responded. "We're going to the penthouse. Wait until you see this."

"Chocola's home?"

"No. One of mine." The General entered the elevator and inserted a card into a panel that contained the numbered floor buttons. When prompted by a green light, he pushed the button for the penthouse, and the two soared to the top of The Elpmet.

Chocola, a seventy-year-old eccentric film director with over forty movies and other varied entertainment projects to his credit, was currently indisposed. No, he wasn't on the toilet. Rather, he was upside-down, face pressed against his balls, hands and feet tied together, on a lawn chair. The chair was as unusual as his contorted body position. This piece of outdoor furniture didn't fit in with the otherwise lavishly appointed 4000-square-foot living room, where Chocola made small spastic movements trying to release himself from the wires that had him hog-tied. The filmmaker's whimpers could not be heard outside the thick walls of The Elpmet's penthouse.

"You can't hear Chocola right now, but I assure you, he is crying," The General offered as he turned a key in the lock, and then inserted a card into a slim slot similar to the one he used in the elevator.

"Wow," was all Karina could say when the door opened. What she noticed first were the walls. She couldn't see the steel, iron, brass, copper, concrete, and brick, the materials that made the walls so massive. What she did see, though, were nearly a hundred varieties of flowers. Daisies. Lilies. Roses. Daffodils. Carnations. Mums. Tulips. Impatiens. Pansies. Geraniums. Marigolds. Hydrangeas. Camellias. Forget-me-nots. Nasturtiums. Azaleas. Hibiscuses. Violets. Peonies. Irises. Goldenrods. Magnolias. Lilacs. Laurels. Bluebonnets. Orchids. Zinnias. And many more. The colors were red and white and yellow and violet,. They were green and purple and blue and pink. The flowers covered every inch of the walls. Chocola, balled and strapped up in the middle of the room, was just a side show. His whining was difficult to decipher from the blasting Indian music that was funneled through metal ceiling grates.

Karina walked deeper into the botanical garden, resting her purse on Chocola's backside, still ignoring his bizarre condition. "These were your choices, General?"

"Oh, no, Karina. They were Chocola's. He personally selected, purchased, cultivated, and then implanted each flower on these walls." The General patted Chocola on the head, a man who had four different variations of flowers stuffed in his mouth, rendering him unable to speak.

"You are an odd little man." Karina paid attention to Chocola for the first time since arriving in the penthouse.

"He's really not little. Chocola is over six feet tall." General McAvoy pulled one of the flowers from his mouth, a purplish type with a name he couldn't quite pronounce. "He just looks tiny, you know, because he's all stuffed up like this."

"Do you have any beer, General?"

"In the ice box."

Karina started to her left where there was an opening to another room.

"In the other direction, honey."

Karina took The General's cue and turned around.

"You see that doorknob, sticking out from the flowers?" The General pointed to an area with a particularly bright collection.

"No, I don't," Karina kept walking in the general direction.

"It's gold. You see it?" The General raised his voice because Karina was now far off in the square footage. He patted Chocola on the head again, and then shook one of his rearranged arms. Chocola glared up at him with puppy dog eyes.

Karina, now fishing around in the flowers, finally located the gold doorknob. "I got it," she yelled back. Then she disappeared.

The General plucked another flower from Chocola's mouth, this one a simple red rose. The thorns from its stem, however, had not been removed and cut up Chocola's inside cheek, gums, tongue, and lips as The General pulled it out. The blood spattering on McAvoy's arms and short-sleeved sweater pissed him off. "Asshole!" The Indian music was starting to annoy him as well. "You are a damn pain in the ass!"

The gold knob turned again, and Karina returned to The General with three ice-cold bottles of Guinness.

"This fool isn't getting one of these beers." The General, with one hand, took a bottle of beer from Karina. With his other, he manipulated a remote control to stop the music.

"What happened to you?" Karina asked, noting the blood on his arms and clothes.

McAvoy nodded at Chocola.

The filmmaker returned the puppy dog eyes and let out a whimper.

Karina sipped her dark beer.

"Alright. Enough bullshit." The General wiped away the blood. "Chocola, I'm untying you."

The seventy-year-old violently shook his head and body, letting out flower-mouthed defiant screams.

"You've had over twenty-four hours. You've been unsuccessful, man." The General attempted to untie him.

Chocola continued his antics, struggling to prevent McAvoy from freeing his bondage. The General, though, was relentless, slamming an elbow into the side of the filmmaker's head and a knee into his gut. A loss of wind deflated Chocola, allowing McAvoy to easily untie him. Once limbs and torso were in normal position, McAvoy yanked the two remaining flowers out of his mouth.

"I could've done it myself! I just needed another three hours!" Chocola was convinced.

"You are not a magician, my friend. You are just a lunatic."

Chocola turned to Karina. "What do you think? I could've got out, right?"

Karina shifted her gaze to The General, then back to Chocola. "I'm sure you can do anything." She picked up the wires that Chocola had used for his self-imposed imprisonment. "Would you like a Guinness?"

"Yes, thank you." Chocola flapped his arm to shake out the numbness that had set in from its day-long restraint. Before he could take control of the alcoholic beverage, however, The General swept in and snatched it away.

"I said none for him. He is being punished." The General lifted Chocola from the lawn chair. "Chocola, tell Ms. Kelly about the Apollo landings. This is what she's here for, not to socialize."

Chocola jogged in place for a moment, another attempt to return his body to a normal state. "They were faked."

"And you know because…why?"

The General smiled. Karina sipped her beer.

Chocola answered, "Because I was the director of the show. I filmed it myself."

"Prove it to me." Karina put down the drink.

"Just look at the footage. We shot it in the desert, right here in California."

"Why come forward now, Chocola? You have so much to lose. Starting with your career. Why now?"

"Because The General asked me to."

Karina looked at her future father-in-law. "General McAvoy is very persuasive, but—"

"No buts. The General saved my life…"

Karina didn't ask how.

"…and he promised continued safety for me. And believe me, that's important. Some people involved with the Apollo landings have already been murdered…killed before they could speak. So of course no one has talked. But now…" Chocola, still bleeding from the mouth, picked up his rose, "I will tell you everything. It's all in the footage."

"I've seen the footage, Chocola. It looks real to me." She nodded to Mitch's father. "You, General?"

"It looked real to me too, but listen to the man…and watch." The General motioned to a screen that was descending upon the flowers. When it stopped, a motion picture started immediately. Karina saw a dark black background. A shady, sand-colored surface. And an Apollo craft was leaving the moon. Flames shot out from the space vehicle as it departed from the ground. Chocola paused the footage.

"I've seen this before. So?" Karina picked up her beer.

"So? So this could not have happened on the moon. Only on Earth."

"Why?"

"The moon has no atmosphere. It is a vacuum. Fire could not be visible in any filming or photography." Chocola moved his arms in circles, still uncomfortable from his hog-tying. He hit "play" and the footage continued, with a still photograph. One astronaut was standing on the moon surface near the American flag. Another was a few feet away. The first astronaut's shadow was very long, nearly four times the length of the alleged space traveler. The other man's shadow was only slightly longer than his seventy-four-inch height. "Note the difference in the size of the two different astronauts' shadows."

Karina nodded.

"These guys are practically right next to each other." Chocola pulled a petal from his mouth. "Natural light could not cause this disparity in the shadows."

"What do you mean by natural light?" Karina asked.

"If you're on the moon, you get light primarily from the sun, and you can get light from earth. Natural light can't cause shadow differences like this. This can only be produced by different lights being used in a film production. In other words, as the director, I fucked up…In many ways, I did. Look at this."

A moving picture began, with hundreds of other clips set to follow. Chocola was prepared to unleash Hollywood's greatest hoax, provable by a monstrous list of filmmaking errors, many, as Karina would see, directly caused by Dylan Travant's father.

Several cocktails down, Laney ordered a Beefeater gin martini with three olives, intending to sip this drink at a slow, dry pace. As the bartender—a Popeye with neither muscle nor spinach—handed her the drink, Spiderman burst through the kitchen door. He swept past Laney, grabbing her Beefeater and taking a manly slug.

Masqueraders pushed aside, Spiderman carefully placed the empty glass on a waiter's tray and turned around to see Batman hot on his trail. Laney, Catwoman to the partiers, trying to protect Spiderman, swatted her long, metallic nails at Batman's mask. The dark armor, though, rejected the attempted scratch, and Batman, with a swift stiff forearm knocked Laney on her ass.

Spiderman, in return, shot a weblike goo material from his wrist, attaching it to the ceiling. The Playboy Bunny cooed and Cinderella danced excitedly, as Spiderman literally used the web to hoist himself to the top of the wall. The other guests watched, some in shock, some in fear, some in amazement, as the superhero angled with an alarming quickness, on the walls and ceiling above them. Batman, however, reacted differently, firing pellets from the base of his right arm. With a certain calmness, he aimed carefully at his comic book partner, rifling off the miniature bullets in systematic, military-like fashion.

His target avoided contact, scurrying from wall to ceiling to wall. Batman, nonetheless, was relentless in his pursuit. Ignoring the growing screams of the people surrounding him, he shot his own wall-climbing device, a suction cup connected to sheetrock, and with seemingly inhuman strength, Batman ripped himself into midair acrobatics. Employing a somersault-like maneuver, he kicked Spiderman in the head, causing the arachnid to lose his balance and fall to the floor. Batman then joined him on the ground, once again knocking down an interceding Catwoman.

Gasps let out and a woman yelled, "Batman is revealed!"

The creature of the night had removed his mask. It was Mitch.

"It's Senator McAvoy!" Charlie Chaplin screamed.

*God, he's hot,* Laney thought.

Spiderman, now completely through a roll, was on his feet and running back toward the kitchen.

"It's Dylan Travant!" Mitch warned. "Get out of my way!"

As Catwoman crawled in the opposite direction, Mitch raced after Spiderman who, in an unexpected turn, blasted through a 4x4-foot framed painting of former Egyptian President Anwar Sadat, leaving a black hole left in the artwork's place. Mitch nonetheless dove in, following his foe.

# Eleven

The media frenzied. Here was a multifaceted story of political intrigue, bravery and sheer mystery. The night of the New Hampshire election, the nation's second presidential primary, Senator Mitch McAvoy was not in that cold New England state. In fact, he wasn't in the United States at all.

Instead, after an early morning press conference, he had flown to the Middle East. From there, he conducted dozens of midday interviews from what appeared to be a Concord, New Hampshire Hilton. Everyone thought he had taken ill, resulting in the lounge and hotel suite satellite correspondences. But no, the Senator was on a totally different continent, involved in a secret coup to capture an international criminal mastermind. Simply, was this positive for the presidential hopeful's campaign? Or was it negative?

The President claimed that Mitch was really a CIA operative. Worse, a vigilante, wrought on personal revenge for his family's business. Her team spun a story of a renegade. A man with war and violence in his blood. A man who wouldn't be there for the American people. Mitch McAvoy, they said, was more concerned with personal vendettas. If that meant trekking to Afghanistan and leaving the USA behind, he would do it now, and would do it later as Commander in Chief.

Unfortunately for The President, however, the American and international, media didn't buy it. Television commentators, radio talk-show hosts, newspaper editorial writers, and internet bloggers again branded Mitch a hero.

To many, Mitch wasn't only seeking justice against a familial villain. Dylan Travant had stolen from millions of Americans, and millions of others from nations around the world. These pundits also argued that it was one of Dylan's gang members, Mario Leggetti, who had shot at The President. In essence, Mitch was seeking justice for The President, his own political adversary.

Other media brass drew a different, but still positive, story. A provocative, sexy tale of chivalry. A battle between two medieval characters. Robin Hood, or Dylan, on the one hand. King Arthur, or Mitch on the other. To them, Dylan Travant was not an evildoer. He stole from the wealthy, yes. But they were covered by insurance. And by all accounts, he had many times given to the poor. These reporters published interviews from hundreds of poverty-stricken human beings, from North America and abroad, who told of Dylan's monetary generosity. The man had lifted so many, by way of gifts of cash, from the streets of trash and sickness, replacing their economic and societal doldrums with stability and happiness.

Dylan's giving notwithstanding, he remained a criminal. To these members of the press, Mitch was righteous in his pursuit. Anarchy would prevail, they posited, if the rule of law was not enforced. So, here was Mitch McAvoy, a senator and presidential candidate, rightfully in hot pursuit of this infamous filmmaker-turned-thief. Bravo to his efforts. How refreshing to see a leader who put justice above politics.

The people, as usual, followed the media's lead. And everyone waited, with bated breath, for the next chapter in this international game of cat and mouse. For surely, it was not over. Mitch was unable to capture Dylan. After sailing through hundreds of yards of piping and duct work, Mitch reported that he landed in an large, elegant swimming pool. The one located outside the hotel lounge where he had conducted the "New Hampshire Primary" interviews earlier that day. By the time he swam to the surface, Dylan had entered a jeep, conveniently stationed just feet from poolside, for his getaway.

Mitch mixed five pounds of ground Kobe beef with two medium yellow onions in a large, clear glass bowl. He added bread crumbs, grated Parmesan cheese, salt, pepper, tarragon, and the specialty of the recipe, sour cream. With his bare hands he rolled and mashed and manipulated the beef mixture until he was satisfied with the texture.

"These will be the best gourmet hamburgers you ever had. I guarantee it," Mitch assured his diners—Karina, The General, Barkstone, and Withermint.

"I'm sure," Withermint responded, watching the Senator form burger patties, and wondering why he was having a barbecue instead of stumping on the campaign trail.

"Uh, Mitch," Barkstone tepidly inquired, "are you heading to Mississippi later today?"

"No." He looked at The General, "Dad, do you think these are too small?"

The General picked up one of the burgers, eyed it carefully, and then said, "No. Perfect."

"I thought so." Mitch molded a sizable round one, and then handed a tray of twenty-plus sour cream, gourmet hamburgers to Karina. "You grill, of course."

Barkstone couldn't understand the gravity of the approaching meal, but he did enjoy watching a presidential candidate mix up raw meat. "That hurricane damage in Mississippi warrants your attention, Mitch. It's massive. You're going to be asked why you didn't show."

“I’m going to Mississippi, Bob, and to four other states in the next week, including Texas.”

“Yes, Texas. Most important, Texas.” Karina, who was still holding the tray, put it on a marble countertop.

“Houston’s a wonderful city, isn’t it, Mitch?” The General indulged in a healthy sip of a full-bodied Spanish red wine.

“Mitch, Karina.” Barkstone shifted his glance from one to the other. “I’ve been thinking about this. You have to lay to rest this nonsense about the moon. You could seriously make fools of yourselves.” He looked to Withermint. “You agree, don’t you, Stella?”

“I don’t know. What information do I have?”

“You have none…yet.” Karina hoisted two huge folders from a briefcase.

“This is madness. It’s one thing to attack The President for not keeping her promise to bring us back to the moon. But it’s another to report that we’ve never been there. We’re credible reporters. Not conspiracy theorists.” Barkstone poured down some of his own wine.

“You should listen to Karina. She’s got my ear about this now, and I’m acting on it. What do you think I was doing in Afghanistan?” Mitch began slicing a shallot. “Off the record, of course.”

“Visiting troops. A good political move,” more wine for Barkstone, “that turned into another superhero episode when you ran into Dylan Travant.”

“Wrong. I didn’t run into him. I knew he was going to be there.”

“That’s not what you told the press…the American people.” Barkstone was indignant.

“I didn’t tell anyone anything.” Mitch was referring to the fact that, until this point, he had had his press secretary speak on his behalf about the episode. Mitch reported to him. He reported to the media. And the media reported to the public.

Withermint was silent. The General and Karina too. But not Barkstone. "This is nonsense. What is the relevance of Dylan Travant and The President's plan to take us back to the moon?"

Mitch was hardly moved by Barkstone's growing agitation.

"If you don't want the story, you can leave." Mitch motioned to the door. "But if you do want it, there are two conditions."

Barkstone listened.

Mitch peeled another shallot and picked up a long knife.

"First, the two of you will write the story." He pointed the cutting instrument at Barkstone and Withermint. "Not Karina."

Withermint, coyly, "and the second condition?"

"The story can't be written until after the upcoming alleged moon landing." Mitch sliced the vegetable in half. "Do we have an agreement?"

"I don't even know if there is a story to write." Barkstone was still incredulous, but less abrasive.

"But if there is?" Mitch pointed the knife again.

"Well," Barkstone talked into the air, not making eye contact with Mitch, "of course. Yes. You have my word on that. You may be President of the United States." Barkstone glanced at the knife. "You have my word…I agree."

"I'm in." Withermint was eager, "Tell me some facts."

Karina sifted through an overstuffed green file and randomly pulled out a photograph. She dropped it on the table in front of Withermint.

The senior reporter looked at the basically uneventful picture. It was the grainy, sandy surface of the moon, featuring one rock.

"There's the letter *C* on this rock, is that the point?"

"Yes," Karina answered.

"So?" the skeptic, Barkstone, chimed in.

"Wait for the lady to explain," The General ordered.

"It's a perfect *C*. I know what you're thinking, Bob. Maybe an astronaut carved his initial or that of his wife or mother or sister. Or maybe it was caused by nature." Karina picked up the photo "But none of those is the case. It's implausible that a natural act formed that perfect letter, that's one in a million, a—"

"Okay." Barkstone gently took the *C*-stone photo from Karina.

"Maybe one of the astronauts *labeled* the rock with the letter *C* for cataloging purposes."

Mitch gently removed the photo from Barkstone's hands. He had already gone over these points with his fiancée. "No, that's not true either. The astronauts, when asked about it, had no answer. Neither for this little issue nor for dozens and dozens of other and, in many cases, much bigger issues." Mitch handed the photograph back to his fiancée.

"But Chocola," Karina began, "the famous film director, he had answers…and proof."

The potential future First Lady re-engaged her green file and, determined to prove the great moon hoax to her colleagues, over the next three hours presented a bank of compelling evidence.

For this freshman dissertation, she continued with the still photos and video footage. There were so many scientifically unexplainable shots. For example, the two Earths seen in footage shot by Buzz Aldrin during the Apollo 11 mission. After this flying cameraman filmed what appeared to be Earth, he manipulated the lens and focused on fellow astronaut Mike Collins, who was located in a different part of the spacecraft. The footage showed what appeared to be a transparency of the Earth taped to a window behind Collins. But it got better. Incredibly, as the camera panned left, behind Neil Armstrong, a second Earth was witnessed.

Chocola had demonstrated to Karina, who now explained to Withermint and Barkstone, that not only was it obvious, even to a layman, that two Earths do not exist, but also that the timing of this filmmaking was a fraud. Allegedly, the moon travelers were thirty-four-plus hours into the Apollo 11 trip at the time of this videotaping. They claimed to be deep in space. However, in part of the footage, it was revealed that they were still low in Earth's orbit, as beautiful blue sky was viewed outside one of the windows.

Then there was the crosshairs issue. The manufacturer of the Apollo cameras had built in crosshairs—reticles placed on the film to aid in calculating distances. These crosshairs would be visible in each and every photo taken on the moon. Yet, they were invisible in many shots. Karina imparted to the group how Dylan's father, the hoax's leading special effects editor, had tampered with the photos to remove other, more glaring defects. Though he was successful in that task, the unexpected result of that tampering was that the crosshairs disappeared. No one caught it until after the photographs had been published to the public.

Another unforeseen photography blunder not taken into consideration by the senior Travant involved the astounding moon temperature variations, which ranged from -180° to over 200° Fahrenheit; astronauts moved back and forth from extreme cold to severe heat. Even today, Karina explained, there is no film stock in existence that could withstand such drastic changes in temperature. The film would have perished. Yet there were scores and scores of still photos and rounds and rounds of video footage shot during the Apollo missions.

Karina told of many other anomalies, including unexplainable reflections in Buzz Aldrin's visor, vast lighting differences among video footage and still photos that had supposedly been shot simultaneously, and astronauts moving at Earth speeds and taking Earth-like steps when they were supposedly walking in one-sixth moon gravity that would enable them to jump nearly twelve feet into the air.

Karina's favorite, though, was the lack of stars in any of the lunar photography. With no atmosphere to obscure sightings, surely there would be thousands of brilliantly lit stars in the pictures and video. However, there were almost none. This was because any credible professional astronomer would easily be able to calculate that the distances between the stars and the moon were inaccurate. Accordingly, because these pictures were fakes, actually taken from Earth, Chocola had instructed Arthur Travant to remove the stars from the film.

NASA, naturally, couldn't explain any of this. Instead, the government agency employed muscle tactics against the naysayers, threatening them with legal action, publicly humiliating them with labels of "lunatics" and "crazies," or causing career destruction. Television networks, radio stations, magazines, newspapers, and book publishers were all strongly discouraged from covering the photography debacles and, as Karina explained, the other substantial evidence proving the phony Apollo missions.

By the end of the Pulitzer Prize winner's recitation, Withermint and even Barkstone were convinced that Karina had met the "By the Preponderance of the Evidence" standard. They wanted to hear more. Especially the specifics of Dylan Travant's involvement…and that of The President.

Mitch cautioned, however, that evidence was still being amassed.

Not in the West Wing. Nor in the East or North. But in the South Wing—that's where, packed away in the furthest reaches of The President's Washington, D.C. mansion, lay the leading lady's favorite room. This four-cornered space in the White House, though, wasn't anyone else's favorite area. And it wasn't at all white. The President had this room painted completely pink.

The walls, ceiling, and floor, all pink. The furniture, pink. The decorations and accessories, pink. Even the phone and computer were pink.

Wearing a pink pant suit, The President leaned against one of her pink walls and smoked a pink cigarette. She sipped not straight scotch or vodka, but a Pink Lady. She looked into a pink-framed mirror and noticed her pink eyeliner and lipstick. Then she took another sip of her Pink Lady.

The White House staff privately, and the press publicly, had speculated about The President's reasons for creating The Pink Room. The predominant theory was that she was attempting to stay in touch with her feminine side. Being The President, a traditionally male role, required certain unusual transitions. The President, so frequently acting in this masculine capacity, needed an outlet to maintain her femininity. Thus, The Pink Room, a self-designed psychological pacifier.

An offshoot hypothesis was that The President had the room built to make it *appear* that she was feminine. Here, a stunt to alleviate her stiff, cardboard—and manly—persona.

Other guesses, though less accepted, were that: pink was her favorite color or a symbol of women's power. A few just figured The President was a weirdo. Whatever her motivations, the room was constructed to her exact specifications, and it was the White House location where she spent most of her time.

A final drag on the pink cigarette, and The President flicked the butt at Laney, who was sitting in a pink chair in front of the pink computer. She did it, not to be cruel, but because she wanted to get the younger lady's attention. "Wake up."

"Yes, Madam President."

"Get that Dylan Travant on that screen. I want him to know that Mitch McAvoy has information tying his father to an Apollo hoax." There had been a pillow talk leak to Laney and therefore to The President.

“Obviously Mitch knows quite a bit, Madam President.”

“Just get Dylan in this room.” She pointed to the pink monitor with a pink pen she had just picked up from a pink desk.

Laney motioned to a pink couch behind her pink computer station. “For your security, you don’t want to be anywhere near this.” Laney referenced the pink webcam.

“Correct.” The President retreated to the pink couch, and turned on another pink monitor, one lacking a webcam, but which was networked to Laney’s computer.

The President lit another pink cigarette and smoked up an inch of ash while Laney went through the complicated procedures to reach Dylan. In the midst of the cancer stick, Dylan’s voice beat through the gray haze. The President waved away the smoke to see him, completely naked, on her twenty-inch monitor. She was, of course, unaffected by his nudity.

Laney, already aroused, unbuttoned her blouse.

“Not enough. All of it, off. Now,” Dylan commanded.

Laney didn’t bother to seek the consent of The President. She had to do what was necessary for this matter of national security. So she peeled off her clothes and quickly was as bare as Dylan. Equally uninterested in Laney’s buff physicality, The President waited impatiently for the dialogue to begin. The discourse started simultaneously with Dylan stroking his lengthy penis and Laney fondling her large breasts.

*This is bizarre,* an ironic Presidential thought.

“General McAvoy, Mitch, and his slut fiancée,” Laney pinched a nipple, “know your father was one of the masterminds behind the faked moon landings.”

“Is that the pot calling the kettle black?” he asked, obviously referring to the *slut* comment.

The President snickered.

With no response from Laney, Dylan continued, penis in hand. “Chocola is of no concern.”

Laney stopped touching herself. “You know he told all?”

“Please put your hand in your crotch.”

Laney obeyed.

“You are not the only one privy to information.” Dylan, employing a Christian Ranieri technique, panned his camera up, providing Laney, and The President, a close-up of his hand-and-cock tandem. “Chocola is a silly, old man. He’s a has-been. There is no credibility in what he says.”

“Well, he provided a lot of specifics, and…” Laney was rather wrapped up in herself, “I’m concerned.”

Dylan’s hand-and-cock responded, “You? You mean The President?”

“I mean…me.”

Dylan manipulated the lens, returning to a wide shot. He ceased the sexual activities. “Put a shirt on.”

Laney momentarily failed to comply, continuing in her quest to orgasm.

“Put a fucking shirt on, Laney!”

The operative acquiesced, lifting her blouse from the pink floor. “There’s concern. Mitch clearly is aware of what you’re up to in Afghanistan. For Christ’s sake, he was there.”

“Watch this, Laney.”

Dylan, suddenly, was gone. The scene cut to the interior of a tent.

Four blond European-looking men crowded around two dark-haired European men. As the shot came closer, the two dark-hairs were revealed to be Italians. The blonds’ heritage was still indiscernible. Their actions, however, were quite apparent. Rapid, continuous punches into the stomachs, chests, and heads of the Italians, who were chained to a pole in the middle of the tent. There was no sound, only picture.

Dylan, in control of the camera work, moved into extreme close-ups. Blood gushed from one man’s nose, which was clearly broken. Red poured just as fast from the mouth of the other beating victim. Then, whilst still in the tight shots, pliers entered the scene. Laney and The President watched as teeth were systematically removed from their agonized faces.

"Enough, Dylan. I get the point." Laney's voice had no emotion. She just wanted to return to their conversation.

A voiceover from Dylan: "No, I don't think you do. These two hit men—I guess that's what you call them—came from Sicily to Afghanistan to kill me. In fact, they came right to my set…Just after we finished the shooting of your President's moon landing and all of the expedition's related bells and whistles…We filmed the collection of a lot of moon rocks…Some real colorful stones."

The President flicked a pink eyelid, a sign of excitement that her moon trip was complete.

But the beating of the Italian men continued, as did Dylan's speaking. "How did these guys know where we were, Laney? And with such good timing?"

"Well, they obviously were sent by Mitch. He was there to get you."

In a medium close-up, Laney observed the extraction of one Italian's two front teeth.

"Wrong, Laney. That's not Mitch's style. He would've come himself."

"Dylan, Mitch is on to you. Why else would he have gone to the Middle East, ending up at a party with you? That's a little beyond coincidence."

Cut to:

Dylan in jeans and a sweater. "You don't get it, do you, Laney? I tipped Mitch off to the party."

The President dropped her newest pink cigarette.

"What?" Laney zoomed in on her face. "Why would you do that?"

"To beat him."

"Are you insane?"

"Certainly not. Could an insane man accomplish everything that I have?" Dylan bit into a meatball parmigiana sandwich. "Mitch merely knew that I would be at that party because I sent word. He is clueless about our little lunar movie. Yes, he's on a fishing expedition, with his investigative reporter girlfriend interviewing every quack trying to sell a book…but he knows nothing." Dylan took another bite. "Damn, these Italians make a good sandwich."

Laney remained silent, understanding what was next.

"Laney?"

"Yes, Dylan?"

"Since I am aware that Mitch didn't deploy my recently-dead mobster friends, I have to ask you a question."

*Oh shit.* Another Presidential thought.

"Why are you trying to kill me?" Dylan engaged the meatball parm for the final time.

"You know I'm not trying to kill you, Dylan. I did the opposite, didn't I? I tried to stop Mitch from getting to you at the masquerade," Laney reminded him.

Dylan used a white napkin to wipe a small amount of tomato sauce from his lip. "Yes, you did. I'll have to think about this."

The monitor cut out.

# Twelve

Sugar. Spice. And everything nice. That included beer, crushed walnuts, licorice, raisins, gummy bears, and heavy cream. Also, a bowl filled with jelly. Chocola boiled it all together in a five-gallon pot. His intention was not to eat it. Of course not. Rather, once the concoction was perfectly blended, he would allow it to cool. Then, his friend Sally would baste his naked body with it from head to toe.

This was normal Sunday afternoon fare for the director. He didn't use the day of rest to take a nap or spoil himself with fine weekend cuisine. Nor did he desire to take a relaxing midday drive. Or kick back and watch a football game or other sporting event. Instead, this was Sally's day to spread Everything Nice up and down Chocola's chest, arms, neck, face, and legs, and upon his ass cheeks. Afterward, he generally returned the favor, covering the forty-something lady's back, booty, and bust with the sweet nectar.

Adding cinnamon, nutmeg, and a pinch of fennel, Chocola stirred the pot with several swift turns of his wrist. He placed a cover over the boiling mass when satisfied, allowing an eighth-of-an-inch opening so it could breathe. Then he plucked a few hairs from his ass and chest, a ritual designed to cause himself momentary pain, but even more, a gift he would give to Sally when she arrived.

Chocola turned down the flame, lowering Everything Nice to a gentle simmer. Then he exited the kitchen, prepared to lay face down on a bushel of poison ivy that he had just procured from the Valley, at the outskirts of Los Angeles. He was immediately sidetracked, however, as the doorbell rang. Apparently, Sally was early.

The malls in Washington were as busy as their counterparts in other major U.S. cities and suburbs. They offered much in the way of one-stop shopping. Clothes outlets. Party stores. Cigar shops. Cell phone centers. Varied restaurants and eateries. Appliance, music, book, card, gift, and pet stores. And usually, the products were cheaper at the malls, given the chain nature of the entities selling them.

There were drawbacks to these modern shopping creations, however. The malls and the massive freestanding retailers initiated the pending extinction of the downtown area. Local mom-and-pop stores languished in despair, watching their customer bases slowly but surely whittle away to a few loyal lot. Without the ability to compete, and more so, without the ability to generate the requisite income, many of these local businesses had been forced to shut down. This had led to empty main streets, reduced municipal tax revenue, and accordingly, increases in property taxes. More important, however, towns and cities had lost their character. Neighborhoods, as they formerly existed, just weren't the same without their flourishing downtown shopping centers.

Mario Leggetti, aware of this social phenomenon, watched with feelings of sadness as the men, women, and children of the nation's capital ambled in and out of the city's largest mall. "You know, these kids probably sit in their houses and apartments all day long and play stupid video games. Then, they come to the malls to buy more video games and other junk, with their parents, who are also buying silly crap. Whatever happened to playing football in the street with the kids from around the block? And going into town to get lunch or buy stuff at the five and ten? I miss that, don't you?

"No," Serena Boll answered, fixing her lipstick in the passenger side mirror of the vehicle where the two actors/thieves were sitting.

"Didn't you grow up with a downtown that you now miss? You know, like some fond childhood memory that has been stripped away from you?"

"No." Serena flipped the mirror shut and pointed to the mall. "I want to know what's going on inside there."

Puppies were barking. Kittens purring. Parrots cursing. Turtles, frogs, and fish were swimming. And customers were petting, hugging, and kissing their newfound friends. And the salespeople were selling them. In the back of this D.C. mall pet store, though, something significantly different, and perhaps offensive, was occurring.

"You need to show me your tits before I say anything more." A finger touched a blouse. The blouse touched two bare breasts. The breasts were ready to touch the air. Of course they were, as they were necessary to ensure national security. To secure The President's reelection and thus the continuous world domination of the United States of America. And therefore, the safety of all the Earth's human inhabitants. Laney's propagandized mind synthesized the rationale, and in literally under a second, she removed her blouse to reveal her succulent breasts. "Do you want to put your mouth on them?" she asked.

"Yes." The finger was replaced by a tongue and lips.

The tongue wasn't savory, though. And the lips were thin and brittle. *This sucks*, Laney thought, for a moment, but quickly rebounded into patriotism. "Oh, wow, that feels good."

"It does? I really make you feel good, Laney?" The tongue and lips. "You're so hot!"

Dogs barking in the background. Parrots mimicking patrons. Cash register jingling and clanging.

"Laney, take off your skirt."

The CIA operative gave a seductive low moan and ran her hand through the stringy hair of her john. "Hold on, Stella, you need to give me something."

"Yes. Some loving." Withermint tugged at Laney's skirt.

Laney gently took the lusting lesbian's hand. "That will happen," she said, slipping down her skirt, "I promise you."

Withermint gazed at Laney, who was now covered only by a metallic blue G-string. The younger woman's face radiated with beauty. Her brain, with manipulation. "I promise you."

Withermint took that as a cue to pull down Laney's panties. Laney, however, took a sexy step back. "Tell me what else Mitch and Karina think about our past moon landings, and our upcoming one. Tell me specifics."

"I will. I promise you that." Withermint took off her own shirt. It wasn't a pretty sight.

"You know, they are idiots, right?" Laney swept a few fingers over her G-string. "This is just politics. Not truth."

"I know," was all Withermint could manage.

"You can take off your…" Laney eyed Withermint's obscene pants, "your trousers."

Withermint quickly removed them and started toward her soon-to-be-lover.

"Not so fast," Laney charmed. "First, you tell …then I show." Laney pulled her thong to the side for a fleeting, but important, glimpse.

Withermint, naturally, began speaking.

The General usually permitted no more than five people in an elevator with him. Not that he was claustrophobic. He had no phobias. Nor psychological disorders of any kind. He wasn't schizophrenic, manic depressive, or even obsessive compulsive. He was never depressed or down. Fuck, the man rarely, if ever, even worried. But he did get angry. And, as far as elevator rides went, it angered him to be overcrowded. Thus, the Rule of Five.

This day, however, his Rule of Five was trumped by his Rule of Ten. Flanked by nine others, The General traveled lightly. His black suit and sunglasses were complemented by only a black pistol. The nine others carried greater artillery. As the elevator soared to the building's highest level, The General uttered only one word. "Dead!"

The electronic door opened, and The General's nine accomplices immediately began a massive spray of automatic gunfire.

Now, with nothing in their way, they entered an empty space that was formerly occupied by a door. Chocola was laid out on the floor, surrounded by thousands of colorful flowers, and was just recently doused in his boiling hot Everything Nice. Unlike any other person in his condition, Chocola was in ecstasy. His captors, moments earlier, had been confused. That emotion, though, was replaced by fear when The General and his army fire-blasted into the penthouse.

It was ten to five, as The General expected. His men instantly killed four of their adversaries. The fifth attempted to raise his firearm, but was thwarted by The General's pistol whipping of the side of his skull. Chocola seemed pleased, as he flipped and slobbered across the floor, covered in third degree burns.

The General continued beating the one living foe until he was content that his assault had resulted in a serious concussion. “I know who sent you. So no need to explain.”

Dazed and unable to answer anyway, the man, a former infantryman himself, looked blankly at the top commanding officer.

“I love it, General. I love it,” Chocola squeaked, assessing his physical depravity, “But I don’t want to die.”

“I told you I would protect you.” The General bounced a few fingers upon his friend’s head, then fired a bullet into the remaining enemy’s left leg. He nodded at two of his underlings, who were dressed in suits similar to the Italian garment worn by General McAvoy. Reacting to their boss’s head movement, they lifted the wounded one from the floor. In tandem, they quickly wrapped a tourniquet—really a curtain they had ripped from a window—around the man’s leg.

“What are you doing, General?” Chocola was confused, pissed. “Kill the motherfucker.”

“Shhh.” The General put an index finger over his mouth. “Let my boys take care of him. Think of him as a prisoner of war.”

Seemingly satisfied, Chocola observed the prisoner, a sad sack with damp red clothes and blackened pride that refused to allow him to scream out the pain he was suffering. Less dazed at this point, the man was aware of his circumstances. “You can kill me,” he blurted out.

“I know,” The General answered. He patted Chocola on the head again, then turned to his subordinates. “Take him to the back and prep him.”

Withermint, as red as her white skin could be, exited the mall in eyeshot of Mario and Serena. The reporter’s rosy cheeks told the entire sex-fest story. She was happy and satisfied. A woman with her desires met, but also a woman who was compromised.

"Figures she's the sellout," Serena noted.

"I would've thought Barkstone," Mario responded. "He's a dry, rotten drip."

"He *is* a nerd, but he does have some integrity…and other interests."

"Who do you think is a better writer, though?" Mario played with the steering wheel, even though the vehicle wasn't operating.

"Who's got the better chops, in your opinion?"

"Who cares." Serena got out of the car because the subject of their stakeout, Laney, had just exited the mall.

"Give her my best," Mario yelled from an open window, then went back to playing with the steering wheel.

Serena was anxious for the confrontation. She was made up to perfection. And she had dressed to impress, wearing a tight one-piece black bodysuit that accentuated every wonderful curve of her standout body. Her ironed-straight light blond hair fell to the middle of her back.

"Is your bush as yellow as that hair?" Laney spoke first, offering a base remark. It wasn't a question meant to be answered.

However, Serena did respond. "I'm not surprised that you're interested. We just saw your girlfriend leave. She was blushing." Serena pointed in the direction of her automobile.

Mario beeped the horn and waved. Neither woman paid him any attention.

"Oh, I remember. You don't have a bush. Completely shaved. Me and everyone else picked that up in *The Great Heist*," Laney smirked. "Whore."

The last comment simply drew an ironic laugh from Serena.

"So, technically, we're now working together." Laney switched to business talk. "Withermint's the mole. What I get from her is coming to Dylan, and…" Laney beamed at Serena,

"I suppose you too. There's no need to conduct your own little investigation." Laney moved in closer to the woman who, not too long ago, had shot her with a stun gun.

"Dylan doesn't trust you." Serena maintained the close proximity.

Laney got even closer. "Dylan likes to see me naked, baby. We have a certain relationship."

Serena double-blinked. "Sex doesn't equate to trust."

Now Laney moved only her lips. "I've been straight with him all the way."

"You cracked him in the head with a gold brick." Serena ignored the lips.

"He embarrassed me with First National. He…Christian… Dylan…same thing…took advantage of me."

A double-blink. Then another one. "No one takes advantage of you, Laney."

"He took advantage of The President."

Serena, with no oral response, reached into her purse. Laney quickly reacted, grabbing Serena's hand.

"No worry." She handed Laney the pocketbook. "Take out what's inside." Double-blink.

Prepared for anything, including a reverse psychology maneuver, Laney passed the purse back to Serena. "You…very slowly." The lips were good, even Serena had to admit. "Remove whatever it is with the tips of your right fingers."

Serena, still merely inches from one of the world's best secret agents, carefully unzipped the bag. With her index and middle fingers, and her thumb, she extracted the lone item from inside. A compact DVD player.

Laney snatched it from the blond bombshell and hit "play." On the screen appeared The Italian President. He looked troubled, and wasn't as cocky as usual.

"Mr. T," he refused to use Dylan's name for obvious reasons, "my apologies for the men from my country that visited you. They haven't returned." The Italian President was in front of a white cloth, so his location could not be ascertained. "I understand, from a meeting with some mutual spiritual friends that you were unhappy with the visit…You are correct that it was at the request of the American." The Italian President turned his head away from the camera, waited a moment, then came fully back into frame. "I will make up for this, as agreed. And we will fulfill the terms of the treaty." The white turned black.

"What *treaty*?" Laney placed the DVD player in her own purse.

"Well, it's a three-way deal." Serena was confident she was in control of the conversation.

"Stop." Laney felt she also had strength. "Just because he implies that The President was behind the assassination attempt on Dylan doesn't make it so."

"Let's put it this way, Laney, Dylan doesn't necessarily think you were in on it." A fine double-blink. "But for The President, it's best that he's out of the way." Another double-blink for good measure. "The treaty, though, should put that salty witch at bay."

*I wish I was naked with Serena instead*, Laney thought, momentarily regressed to her recent nasty deed with Withermint. *At least Serena is hot.*

"Would you like to know the terms?" Serena asked.

"You're not going to release the video of the moon landing? That makes no sense for anyone."

"There is some nice behind-the-scenes footage." Serena flipped her hair. "I did the interviews, you know, for the DVD extras."

"But Dylan would have as much to lose as The President. He's still an artist. He would lose all credibility." Laney was worried, despite her argument.

"Oh, you're right about that." Serena was serious, easing Laney's concern. "Dylan Travant always has considered himself a fine filmmaker."

"So releasing footage from The President's upcoming moon landing isn't part of the treaty?"

"Of course not. Do you think Dylan would want to help Mitch McAvoy's cause?"

Laney shook her head. "Then tell me the terms."

Double blink.

# THIRTEEN

"Not long after sunrise, the handcrafted oak wheels of a heavy horse-drawn carriage clattered against the hard frost-bitten dirt road that channeled the vehicle-of-the-day from its usual barnyard garage to the local house of worship. Sheltered from the cool December morning air, a petite, attractive middle-class mother knitted a sweater for her teenage child, Sarah, who slept undisturbed despite the carriage's rumbling. Sarah's father, an educated farmer, read the Sunday paper, scowling at an editorial that supported a political movement which threatened to end his livelihood. No one talked, though, conforming to a family tradition. Conversation could only commence at breakfast, after the family returned from church.

"Aside from their Sunday morning silence, Sarah's family was the picture of normal. Her parents were in love with each other, as well as loyal to their marital vows. They argued from time to time. Sometimes over money. Sometimes over nothing. The family took trips to the beach in the summer and visited the city at least once a season. They shared laughter with friends and family. They attended church every Sunday and sang with the other parishioners. Sarah played with friends from school—she even played with the children of her parents' slaves. *That was normal.*

"Sarah's parents, like her grandparents and great-grandparents, owned colored people. Sarah was taught by her parents, and the laws that governed them, that slavery was not only legal, but also moral. The socialization of the economic and principled value of owning other human beings began shortly after Sarah's birth. Slaves were all around her; the infant's subconscious mind was propagandized by their subservient presence. When the child was old enough to understand spoken language, she was told by her parents and her friends' parents that slaves were not human beings in the same sense as white folks. As Sarah grew older, educators, intellects, and leaders reaffirmed her upbringing. The lives of Negroes were not as valuable as the lives of Caucasians. In fact, their *lives* weren't really valuable at all. Ownership of slaves—as property—was a constitutional right. A few Supreme Court justices even said so.

"Sarah was told that her parents and her friends' parents could do whatever they wanted with their property. And so it went. And so it was legal, and normal in her society, when the father of Sarah's best friend decided to destroy one of his pieces of property. He shot and killed Old Willie, a slave, because it wasn't economical to have him on the plantation any longer. Sarah was confused by the pointless killing, but accepted it. Although she was taught that Negroes should only be terminated in rare circumstances, it was indeed lawful.

"The entire institution of slavery was moral in Sarah's world. In fact, at least fifty percent of the nation agreed with that proposition. As Sarah grew into adulthood, not only did she agree, but she owned slaves of her own. She never became aware that Negroes were human beings.

"Most who believe in the alleged constitutional right of abortion have been crafted out of the same mold as pro-slavery activists from early America."

*Whoa...Shit. Didn't see that coming.* Mitch, at the second CNC primary debate, shot a smile at the twenty-five-year-old Michigan graduate student who was apparently about to draw a parallel between slavery and abortion.

*What the fuck is this nonsense?* The President grimaced.

Kassie Conci, an English doctoral candidate, continued, "These are misguided souls, unwittingly educated by prior generations of the misguided. Their thoughts are a lethal concoction of shallow, self-serving ancestral influence. Yet, these are not evil people. They only become evil if they become aware that in aborting a pregnancy, they are killing a human life—or even that they *may* be killing a human life.

"Pro-abortion activists, like their forefathers, have the law on their side. Five Supreme Court justices—five people—have told them it is legal to terminate a pregnancy. It is legal to kill a fetus. It is legal to crush the fetus' skull and brain and then dump the former life into a trash can. With lawyers and judges, politicians and social leaders, and parents, relatives, and friends telling children that abortion is legal, and thus moral, the children naturally come to believe that abortion is a justifiable act. A terrible cycle of thoughtlessness and denial ensues in the same manner that it did with supporters of slavery."

*This girl is hot.* Mitch pictured the coed in her underwear.

"The majority of people who support abortion are not stupid, morally corrupt or even callous. They simply have been socially engineered not to think; they're resting on a cleverly created crutch of convenience. Artificially constructed 'constitutional' terms like 'privacy' have been embedded in their psyche and buttressed with ironic phrases such as 'reproductive rights.' But now think..."

*You think, you smarmy little bitch. Women can do whatever they want with their bodies.* The President thought about Laney as an example.

Kassie looked at The President, deadpan, and went on. "Some people *just know* that human life is created upon conception; it is innate knowledge that they have within themselves. For those who struggle, though, and do not *just know*, there is enlightening comfort in the fact that scientists cannot prove that a fetus—at any stage—is *not* a human life. It is impossible to be certain that a fetus is not a human being. Would any intelligent, moral person kill a fetus if he or she is not sure if the fetus is a human life?"

The President wanted to answer, but Kassie beat her to it.

"Of course not. Most of those who are pro-choice are indeed not morally corrupt; they just haven't thought of this before."

Mitch was now thinking of Kassie naked from the waist down. She was just about to remove her bra…

In the real world, though, the grad student took a sip of ice water and headed into her conclusion. "There are those abortion advocates who conjecture that at a specific point in a pregnancy, the fetus miraculously turns into a human being. This notion is presumably based on timetables of when the fetus can live on its own, outside of the womb. In their opinion, abortion should only be legal until this magical human transformation has occurred. The problem, however, is that the timetable keeps changing with medical advancements. In one decade, a fetus could not survive outside the womb at four and a half months old. Now, the same age child can be delivered and live until one-hundred. Perhaps they weren't human beings in the 1970s, but with the millennium came papers of life? For this thoughtful bunch, what can they do about all of the premature aborted babies? Nothing—but they can conjecture that in twenty-five years from now, or maybe even ten, a child will be able to live outside the womb at an even earlier timetable than current science permits. No one wants to take a chance of killing a child, right?" Kassie was on a roll.

"Anti-abortion activists are difficult to reason with; the re-education didn't work with them. Like abolitionists before, pro-lifers have innate knowledge that atrocities against humanity are legally being committed in their supposedly just environment. In 1850, it was clear to some that slavery was immoral. For others, they suffered in a muddled mess of handed down confusion and bedlam. Today, the divide over life wreaks similar unfortunate havoc. But those Sarahs who want to think, can do so. Saving human lives, and personal moral conviction, is only a thoughtful consideration away."

Kassie again looked to the woman who was currently leading the free world. "Madam President," she outstretched her arms, "How do you respond to this?"

*Fuck, why the hell is she going to her first?* Mitch consoled himself, *Maybe she'll give a stupid answer.*

"First, Kassie, I want to commend you on a well-thought out argument. You are indeed an intelligent young lady who has much to look forward to."

*Damn it, that was good. And she used her first name.*

"However," The President made direct eye contact with the twenty-five-year-old, "There are at least fifty percent of our American brothers and sisters who think that women have an absolute constitutional right to choose. And I don't think this private, personal matter is equivalent to the macro atrocities of slavery." The President outstretched her arms to Kassie, and then to the cameras and her American constituents.

Mitch nodded at Kassie, formulating a precise, electrifying response. He just needed The President to shut her mouth, and he would deliver charismatic words of political and Biblical mastery.

Lincoln had a beard with no mustache. Washington had wooden teeth—or was that a fallacy? Teddy Roosevelt had the

Rough Riders. Clinton, well, he had the women. As did JFK. Reagan, he had Hollywood. And FDR had the New Deal. But what did The President have?

Laney surveyed The Pink Room. And she counted. She was into numbers, always had been. Numerology was a hobby of hers. So, she counted every damn item in the room. Nothing in groups. Everything was to be assessed as a separate, unique item. Even the pens, pencils, and paper clips. By the time The Defense Secretary arrived, Laney had counted 1,032 pink items.

"This is The President's beard with no mustache," Laney proclaimed.

"What?" The Defense Secretary was confused.

"It's her wooden teeth…her Hollywood and Rough Riders."

"Laney, what the hell are you talking about?" The Defense Secretary had passed into being baffled.

"When I finish my count, I'm sure there will be over two thousand pink items in this room." Laney added up a few more pieces. "You know what I mean?"

"No," The Defense Secretary was becoming annoyed. "You saw the debate?"

Laney interrupted herself. "Yes…And I had no idea that Mitch was pro life."

"He is?"

"Well, you heard him, didn't you?"

"I heard him talk in circles of wizardry, saying not much of anything substantive." The Defense Secretary looked, curiously, at a pink cactus that The President used as a paperweight.

"He said that he didn't want to see babies killed."

"So, nobody wants to see babies killed." The Defense Secretary picked up the cactus. It pricked his finger. "Ahh!…Can we get to the point!"

Laney handed the man with the dark eyes a pink tissue to stop his bleeding. He ripped it from her hand.

"The Vatican is more and more convinced that The President was behind Dylan in *The Great Heist*," Laney began.

"The President had nothing to do with that fucking theft. She's tried to have Dylan killed twice now. For Christ's sake, she commissioned The Italian President to have the deed carried out."

"The Vatican thinks it was a ploy." Laney glanced at the parakeet that she had clipped from the mall pet store. She painted it pink for The President. The bird was chirping nonsense.

"This is a disaster." The Defense Secretary tossed his tissue into a petite, pink garbage can. His finger had stopped bleeding.

"And they're real sympathetic to the McAvoys now." Laney turned to the parakeet, "Quiet!" Then back to The Defense Secretary. "After all, they were victims just like the Church."

"Yeah, I get it. Mitch's nemesis, Dylan Travant, robbed him and the Pope...But it's absurd to think The President was involved."

"Unfortunately, that's what Dylan told The Italian President and the Vatican."

"God damn it!" The Defense Secretary slammed his fist into the desk, causing the bleeding to begin again, as well as the bird chirping.

"The President did select Dylan to fake the moon landings. It doesn't look good," Laney shot a look at the parakeet, "Shut up, honey."

"What do they want, Laney?"

"Aside from The President's death?"

"This is no joke."

"No, it's not." Laney took a chair.

"They've proposed a treaty. It involves everyone. And it will save The President's career...and life."

This wasn't the first treaty forced by the Vatican. So The Defense Secretary became matter-of-fact. "The terms?"

"Dylan's next movie must be a pro-Christ flick."

"That's his problem. What do we have to do?"

"Well, here's the easy part. Dylan gets $500 million."

"Done. We'll take it from the CIA."

"Ahh…I don't know about that."

"You don't need to know, Laney." The Defense Secretary showed the darkest of his eyes "It will be done. Now, what are the real terms?"

"It's much graver than we've ever seen before." Laney exited the chair, staring intently into those dark eyes, "They want the next Supreme Court Justice. They want *Roe v. Wade* overturned. They want abortion outlawed in the United States. They want, as they put it, morality."

"What?"

"Hey, they *are* Catholics."

"But how? There's no vacancy on the bench."

"Somebody's got to go." Laney stared into a blank face. "Look, I'm as pro-choice as you. It's up to a woman. I've had an abortion myself, but—"

"I don't give a shit about a woman's right to choose," The Defense Secretary cut Laney off. "This is political suicide. If The President appoints a pro-lifer, she's finished. She'll lose her entire base. She'll lose the election."

"The Vatican has apparently considered that. It's not a problem."

"How's that?"

"She can appoint Mitch." Laney gently picked up the cactus. "And make him the Chief Justice."

# FOURTEEN

There can be no ties in a political election. One way or another, one person ultimately is going to win. For now, though, Mitch and The President were in a dead heat. She had her strategy for victory, and he had his.

Both had entered the race with bulging war chests of donations. The President, at first, had the monetary advantage, as she was the incumbent. The national delegation had supported her pending re-election bid for some time. No one had expected a primary battle, and, thus, all of the money was directed to her. When Mitch announced his candidacy, however, things changed—though it took some work.

Party leadership, from state to state, initially was reluctant to publicly throw their weight behind the young Florida senator. It was unusual for a sitting president to have an intraparty challenge for a second term, and The President was powerful. Conventional wisdom was that anyone, including the polished and heroic Mitch McAvoy, would have very little chance in upsetting the woman. Congressmen, senators, governors, state legislators, and behind-the-scenes party bosses were rightfully concerned that supporting

Mitch McAvoy would lead to their own political demise. So they needed to be convinced.

The first demonstration of Mitch's ability to succeed was his own massive bankroll: there was already millions in place. And quickly, in an absolutely mind-boggling manner, he raised millions more. This was impressive, and a number of top politicians joined his bandwagon. The list grew rapidly, spurred on by the energy and strength of Senator Justin Keller. The senior Florida lawmaker controlled much in the way of national fundraising. He had raised substantial dollars for elected officials, on all levels, across the country. Now, it was not only time for them to show their loyalty to Keller and endorse Mitch, but to dip into their campaign coffers and donate.

Then came the celebrities. Mitch, holding the star himself, was surrounded by many others. Actors, filmmakers, entertainment executives, singers, and songwriters. One after the other spoke words of praise about Mitch McAvoy, and how the United States of America would regain international respect with this man at the helm. The press, of course, capitalized on the fanfare, and, not so subtly, rallied around the McAvoy campaign.

One element benefited the other. Cash drew political support and vice versa. Celebrity backings raised cash, as did the media love-fest. An Indiana senator signing on meant two Ohio congressmen coming on board, which resulted in three press conferences, 88 television reports, several hundred thousand dollars in donations, five movie star outcries, another million dollars, two governors joining the ranks…and so on…and so on…and so on…and so on. The McAvoy campaign strategy embodied the true domino effect of financing, endorsements, and national attention. But it just netted an exact tie with The President. Her following, and campaign contributions, indeed remained strong. Though everyone was now convinced that Mitch could win, each and every state was a battle ground.

Polls were nearly fifty-fifty regardless of demographics, economic status, and educational background. The numbers were even in states that normally voted red, and in those that regularly went blue. It didn't matter if caucuses were held, or if there were ordinary primaries. With ten elections completed, the President had won five, as did Mitch. Something had to give.

Karina, making love to her fiancé, thought about the moon. *This is incredible.*

"Are you thinking about the moon?" Mitch was close to an orgasm.

"You are a genius." Karina was close as well. "Tell me…" she was getting closer, "Tell me." Closer. "Tell—" Orgasm!

Mitch too. "Yes, I love you."

Karina kissed Mitch on the lips. "I love you."

Mitch got up from his Miami home master bed. Karina observed the muscular nuances in the movements of his triceps and trapezoids as he pulled on a pair of dark blue sweat shorts. His chest was massive. *Full of hair*, Karina noted. Mitch was the quintessential man's man. There was nothing metrosexual about him. He was a man through and through, and that's exactly what Karina desired.

"Did you ever think of shaving your chest, Mitch?"

"No."

That was the answer Karina wanted to hear, an affirmative rejection of the tasteless act, without any hesitation.

"Did you ever wear a Speedo?"

"No."

Perfect. "Do you like tennis?"

*I only like contact sports*, Mitch thought, *and other ones that are dangerous.* Mitch looked out to the ocean from a gigantic bay window. "I have no interest in tennis."

Karina's eyes, already bright, sparkled. "Would you ever kiss another guy?"

"Are you fucking nuts?" Mitch turned from the window.

"So what's the answer?" Karina stood, totally naked, beautiful, in front of him.

Mitch's response consisted of dropping to his knees, grabbing Karina by her ass, and passionately kissing the wonderful area between her legs. In moments, she orgasmed again.

"God, I love you." Karina pulled Mitch up from the floor, a pine hardwood. "Can you tell me something about your mother? I want to know what she was like."

Mitch gazed at Karina's face. Nowhere in particular. His look traveled about her mouth, nose, chin, eyes, forehead, hair. Everywhere. He gazed, with no immediate answer, and went back to the bay window. "My mother." He consumed the ocean. "She was me."

"Strong?"

"Definitely."

"Smart?" Karina joined him at the window.

"Brilliant."

"Loyal?"

"The most." Mitch touched Karina's cheek. "She was the most loyal." He revisited the ocean. "That's why she died."

Karina didn't understand. His mother's death was a mystery, even to an investigative reporter. She was willing to let it remain in the annals of silence if that was Mitch's wish. But he decided to speak.

"I was thirteen," he tapped the window with a finger, "thirteen and a half," he tapped again. "My father was overseas, and we… my mother and I…were right there." Mitch tapped the window one more time, referencing the ocean.

"On a boat?" Karina quietly asked.

"On my mother's boat. Just me and her…We weren't far from here. In the Caribbean." Mitch touched Karina's cheek again.

"Look at the water. It's amazing. It appears like it never ends."

"It doesn't end." Karina returned the affection, softly touching Mitch's cheek.

"The boat, as you probably guessed, was very big. A yacht. My mother adored it. It was hers and hers alone. There would be no captain other than her. But, Karina, the woman could navigate that boat. We traveled from sea to sea, island to island, many times, just the two of us." Mitch stopped and peered at the ocean.

"And this time? In the Caribbean?"

"It was just the two of us," Mitch answered, turning from the water. "It was some boat," he turned to the sea again, "Attractive… as was my mother." He tapped the window. "We were attacked… they wanted the boat…and they wanted my mother."

"Pirates?"

"No. It wasn't that random."

"It had something to do with your father?"

"Perhaps…I don't know…he doesn't know…but they knew our names."

Karina took his hand. "How many men were there, Mitch?"

"Three."

Karina was nervous to ask the next question, but she did. "Did they rape your mother?"

"No."

She waited for him to continue.

"It was in the black of night. We were just sort of drifting. I was in my quarters, and my mother was in hers. They must've just pulled alongside us and climbed on. Your basic breaking and entering, like in a house." Mitch led Karina to their bed and sat down. He focused on her eyes. "At first, I thought I was lucky, at thirteen, because my mother immediately shot and killed two of the guys. It was incredible. This thirty-five-year-old woman shot them right in the head. But thirteen was a horrible number for me…because the third one shot and killed her." Mitch stayed with Karina's eyes. "The number was bad for him too, though…I stabbed that motherfucker to death. One time for each of those wicked thirteen years."

"Mitch…"

The man's man kept up with the eyes. "Now let's talk about the number fifty, as in fifty percent, and how reaching for the moon will significantly increase that number for me."

"Yes."

"No."

"No."

"No."

It looked like the affirmative was going to lose. But then—

"Yes."

"Yes."

Now things were equal.

"Yes."

"No."

Yes, things were equal. Not for long, though, as there was one more vote to be cast. The ninth, the swing vote, picked his eighty-one-year-old nose, then flicked the winnings to the floor. His colleagues, all disgusted, uttered nothing. How could they?

*Anything could sway this man,* Justice Carmelo Martinez, the newest to the Supreme Court, thought.

*He's got one foot in the grave and the other on a banana peel,* a more seasoned colleague internally opined.

Phone ringing? During deliberations? The swing judge, Wally O'Malley, picked up. "Hello." Indiscernible dialogue on the other end.

"Sure, I have a few moments." O'Malley turned to the others, "I'm sorry, I need to step out." He ignored the perturbed glares of the other justices, picked another good one, and left the room.

Down the hallway, in an area no one outside the royal nine

dared visit, the conversation continued. It was a discussion of substance; a discourse of supreme authority, corruption, and abuse between The President and one of her three appointees. Her legacy, with a fourth selection imminent, wouldn't be just a return trip to the moon, but also the crafting and shaping of the country's highest court, and thus the law.

The President: "So, what's the vote?" She was referring to the current case, a rare matter of Supreme Court first jurisdiction. A political action committee had filed an order to show cause, seeking an injunction to prevent NASA from sending the expedition to the moon. The PAC argued that Congress had no constitutional authority to earmark funds for travel outside of the Earth's atmosphere. They said that the founding fathers clearly drafted the Constitution with the intent that American taxpayer dollars could only be spent on this planet, and not beyond. Counsel for NASA rebutted that the plain language of the Constitution did not prohibit such an expenditure, and that the document was drafted with the purpose to be flexible for societal, political, and scientific advances that inevitably would occur over time.

Justice O'Malley: "It's a tie,"

The President: "I'm getting sick of ties."

Justice O'Malley: "That's understandable, Madam President."

The President: "So, I've won? The injunction will not be granted?" She knew that O'Malley was the swing vote.

O'Malley: "That's correct. You will have your trip to the moon." O'Malley foolishly thought the landing was going to be real.

The President: "That's just excellent, Justice O'Malley. You are an asset to the Court and the American people."

O'Malley: "Thank you, Madam President." He found his way back into his nose.

The President: "So, give me the rundown."

O'Malley: "Well, Martinez and Blaine immediately voted no." He dug deep, searching. "And with a little jostling from them, Cornish and Tipazella denied the injunction as well."

The President: "What about Williams?"

O'Malley: "Charlotte? Oh, no. She said the billions should be spent on the poor. She voted to grant the injunction."

The President: "That bitch. I appointed her."

O'Malley: "Yes, a bad choice." He again located what he was looking for, and flicked the excretion on the hallway's judicial walls. As it landed, O'Malley noticed a monitor that continuously ticked with the world's most updated news. An Internet alert grabbed his attention as The President was rambling on about Charlotte Williams.

O'Malley: "Madam President, I'm sorry,"

The President: "What?"

O'Malley: "Another injunction has been filed."

The President: "About the moon?"

O'Malley: "No. To freeze your campaign accounts because you received nearly $10 million in donations from criminals. From the thieves in *The Great Heist*."

The President: "Fuck."

The phone went dead. Justice O'Malley picked his nose and strolled back to the deliberations, prepared to send Americans, once again, to the moon.

Karina's backstroke was sound. As was her butterfly and breaststroke. But her greatest strength in the water was freestyle. The propeller movement of her arms acted simultaneously with her furious leg kicking. The splash, actually quite minimal for all her speed, bubbled as the athlete manipulated her face in and out of the water. She took necessary breaths with each stroke, gliding from one end of the pool to the other.

"She's a force of nature." Barkstone admired his writing partner.

"How did she uncover those contributions?" Withermint inquired, smoking a cigarette.

"I don't know." Barkstone accidentally inhaled the second-hand smoke. "You shouldn't do that in here. Karina will be mad."

"Am I supposed to care?" Withermint took another drag. She shot a look at Karina, who was effortlessly continuing with her swim. "You two write up this incredible story, and leave me completely out?"

"You've been working a lot on the moon. And you've got your own stories. You hardly ever bring either of us in." Barkstone was defensive.

"But I don't hide anything from you."

"We didn't hide anything from you, Stella." Barkstone gave a mock, dorky punch to her arm. "Come on, we love you."

Withermint, acting consoled, punched him back. More like slugged him in the shoulder.

"Hey!" Barkstone immediately put pressure on the top of his arm to ease the pain. Karina, oblivious, kept swimming.

"You're not going to let a girl beat you up, are you, Bob?" Withermint patted his other shoulder playfully. "Those videos are devastating."

"Aren't they?" Barkstone smiled, forgetting his arm.

"You've got five of Dylan's crew handing over millions of dollars to The President's top campaign chiefs. On fucking camera! How did Karina obtain this?"

"I have my methods." Karina was out of the pool, hard nipples to be read by the world. Currently, the total population was only Barkstone and Withermint and neither wanted to stop reading. "Awestruck, huh, Stella?" Karina was referencing her reporting.

"Yes." Withermint was referencing her tits. "You've got chairmen in California, Georgia, New York, Vermont, and all over the place, accepting contributions from these thieves."

"And it's all cash," Barkstone chimed in.

Realizing that neither Karina nor Barkstone was going to reveal sources, Withermint decided to praise them. "Very good work."

"Thanks," Karina answered. "Now could you put out that cigarette?"

Withermint could feel that something was wrong. She crushed the flame with her forefinger and thumb.

The President, in a fashionably bright red suit, stood next to The Press Secretary at a White House podium. Symbols of democracy, of the United States, flanked her. A framed dollar bill. A model of the Empire State Building. The Declaration of Independence. A ten-foot version of the Statue of Liberty. A photograph of Abraham Lincoln, beard with no mustache brazenly visible. A portrait of George Washington, wooden teeth not noticeable. A booklet containing the entire contents of the United States Constitution and its amendments. Here, in The President's White House museum, she held the day's necessary press conference.

The leader took questions, the first from a friendly voice. Some D.C. television anchor. "Madam President, you are obviously pleased with the Supreme Court denying the NASA injunction. So when are our men flying to the moon?"

"Men *and* women, Michael." The President's cheeks made their move. "It will be a surprise."

Immediate chatter rattled as several reporters and pundits beckoned for the chance to ask the next question. The President, acquiescing to herself that shit was unstoppable, picked out one she considered an asshole. The greatest of assholes, in fact. "Yes, Ms. Kelly."

"Thank you, Madam President. Can you explain why you accepted about $10 million in cash contributions from criminals?

From thieves who are wanted by," Karina looked at the paperwork in her hands, "over 100 countries, covering every continent except Antarctica."

"Yes." And The President said nothing else. Silence lasted for a few moments, and then the majority of the press corps began to laugh, including Karina.

The Press Secretary interceded. "The President cannot control who donates to her campaign. There are literally hundreds of thousands of individual contributors. It's not as if she personally accepts these donations. She actually knows the identities of less than one percent of her generous supporters."

The Press Secretary nodded at her boss, "and it's crazy to think that she would purposely take money from those who committed The Great Heist. My God, Mario Leggetti shot at her." The Press Secretary singled out Karina with a hand motion,. "You know that Dylan Travant orchestrated this as a publicity stunt and nothing more. He hates The President. He hates America."

"I know that he hates my fiancé. He hates the McAvoys. He stole from them. And he wants to see The President defeat Mitch. Apparently, there is some unholy alliance."

"No, Ms. Kelly, there is just a filmmaker, a thief, playing games." The Press Secretary pointed to another reporter, ready to take the next question. The President's cheeks, again, moved ever so slightly.

There's a cake for every special occasion. Anniversaries, graduations, baptisms, bar mitzvahs, and parties of all kinds. Cakes are there at beginnings, such as births. And at ends, for instance, retirements. Cakes were a favorite of Laney's, not just to eat, but to give as gifts.

She prided herself on the presentation of her cakes. The reason was that if she was bestowing them, it meant she made them herself. Some of these baked goods were frosted, with delicious vanilla, chocolate, or butterscotch toppings. Others were left plain on the exterior, as their moist textures forbade icing. She never used pudding filling or nuts. It was just a matter of taste.

Today, her gift was a banana cake with vanilla icing. The event requiring Laney's baking wasn't a formal party. There was no birthday, holiday, or religious ceremony. Rather, the cake was just a gesture, for consumption at a two-person private gathering. The recipient of the dessert, Withermint, was pleasantly surprised at the offering and invited its creator into her modest two-bedroom Arlington, Virginia condominium. When the door to the unit shut behind Laney, she put the banana cake in Withermint's hands and asked, "Do you have any beer?"

"Sure," Withermint replied. "Many different brands. What kind would you like?"

"Something pale."

"Like The President?" Withermint chuckled.

"Not funny, Stella." Laney took a seat in a leather chair, which was complemented at the other end of Withermint's living room by another similar styled leather chair. In the middle of these two one-seaters was a leather couch. All of the furniture was a dark shade of brown.

Withermint delivered Laney a light German import. "Good?"

"Fine." Laney sipped the drink, "Yes, fine."

"So, why the cake, Laney? Why the beer? Why the unexpected visit? You don't actually like me, do you?"

"No," Laney said. "It's just business." The President's best departed her leather chair and visited her cake, which Withermint had placed on the dining room table. She removed the plastic wrap that had protected her present from the dangerous elements of the outside world. "Do you know how many fresh bananas I used to make this cake?"

Withermint shook her head.

Laney sipped her beer. “Four.,” she sipped again, “ And they were aged, not rotten, but aged.” Another sip, and then…the lips. “Do you know what that means?”

Withermint shook her head, enraptured, already, by the lips.

“It means that this cake is very, very moist.” Laney went to a knife block a few feet away.

Withermint’s eyes trailed her saunter. She trailed the lips.

The lips. “Over here, Stella…” The lips.

Withermint obeyed, arriving at the knife and cake and lips.

Laney sliced.

Withermint moistened with the dessert.

The lips. “Why didn’t you tell me about Karina Kelly’s blasphemous article?” Laney fondled the piece of cake she just cut.

Withermint wanted it. “I didn’t know, Laney. They don’t tell me everything. I think I’ve gotten everything I can out of them.” She melted in the lips. “You’re not disappointed with me, are you, Laney?”

Ripened bananas creamed in Laney’s closing hand as she lifted the cake to lips level. “You’ve told me everything that you know?”

“Yes. Yes I have.”

“Okay. I believe you.” Laney gently opened Withermint’s mouth, feeding her the cake gift.

Over 50,000 people present. Billboards, print and electronic, everywhere. The greenest of grass. And the dirtiest of dirt. Men, dozens of them, in uniform. And items that, in other circumstances, certainly could be weapons. There were hot dogs, popcorn, peanuts, pretzels, and beer. Mitch ordered one up. “Guinness, of course.”. He shook the vendor’s hand, passing him a twenty-dollar bill. “God, I love baseball.”

The St. Louis Cardinals took the field. With their arrival, the crowd roared, standing, including Mitch, Karina, and The General.

"So, you've got that interesting offer." The General popped a few shelled peanuts into his mouth. "Are you pleased?"

"Dad, I don't want to miss the starting lineups." Mitch listened to the announcer's familiar, deep Missouri voice. "The Cards need some more starting pitching. And the National League would be better off with the designated hitter, don't you think?" Mitch was now talking to two of the several Secret Service agents that surrounded him.

A guy two rows behind him answered instead. "You know it, Mitch. You got my vote."

"Me too!" a forty-something wife added, smiling from ear to ear.

"And us, we're with you, Mitch! Screw that hag!"

Mitch stood up to face his supporters,and waved. "Thank you! Thank you!"

At that, the crowd erupted again. A standing ovation, as the fans realized who was watching the ballgame with them. Mitch continued to wave, leaning down to his father and whispering in his ear, "She needs to make this offer public."

Karina, listening in, responded, "That is already being arranged. Whether or not she intended it."

Mitch kept smiling and waving. The crowd kept cheering.

The General returned the whisper. "And she'll be quite unhappy with your rejection."

"And embarrassed." Mitch, still smiling, and with a final wipe of his hand sat down. He sipped his Guinness.

# Fifteen

It was a monumental press day in Washington, D.C. In the United States. Internationally. The public learned everything that Mitch and his confidants knew the day before.

First, three-year Supreme Court veteran Charlotte Williams had been found guilty of heroin possession when she was a college freshman. She lied about the conviction on her law school application and in her bar admission forms. The woman, who since that troubled time had orchestrated a meteoric rise to law's greatest heights, including a stint as a California U.S. Attorney and ultimately a seat on America's top court, was just found to be in possession of crack cocaine. FBI agents posed with the rocky white substance for a gaggle of reporters and cameras. Williams was scheduled to hold a press conference later in the day, announcing her immediate resignation from the robe.

The news didn't stop there. Bob Barkstone broke the related story that The President was being pressured by The Vice President and members of Congress to appoint the most qualified replacement for Williams—undefeated trial lawyer and Renaissance Man intellectual Mitch McAvoy. Preliminary reports indicated that the Senator and presidential candidate was interested, because his greatest concern was seeking justice.

But there was more shocking—and this time, sad—reporting by Barkstone. His colleague and friend, Stella Withermint, had been found dead in her Virginia apartment. At only forty-five years old, the award-winning reporter had suffered a sudden brain aneurysm.

The polls reflected the political chaos suffered by The President. She hit a nine-point slide, courtesy of *The Great Heist* political contributions and the drug bust of a woman she had championed for a Supreme Court lifetime appointment just a few years earlier.

On the other hand, The President had protected her livelihood, in dual terms. The Vatican was initially satiated by the timely, coincidental judicial resignation and the prospect that the vacant seat would be filled by an anti-abortion barrister.

"You were up by three points, with the moon injunction victory. Now you're down six," the Defense Secretary presented the facts. "This isn't a catastrophe."

"It is if I name some pro-life asshole to replace Williams." The President turned to her scotch. "Then I'm done! But Mitch… we could perhaps negotiate that he doesn't vote pro-life until after the election's over. He's got to know that, no matter what, he can't beat me. Dylan aside, he just can't beat me."

"How did Barkstone know that we were considering Mitch?" The Defense Secretary beckoned Laney with the dark eyes.

"You read the article," she replied, refusing to state the obvious—The Vice President *et al*.

"Hmmm." Dark eyes. "Stella Withermint surely wasn't available to help us with a little pre-notice."

"Yes, unfortunately she had an unexpected passing." Laney turned to The President. "Dylan will keep to the treaty. Your trip to the moon will happen, with no interference, and your poll numbers will bounce."

The President fingered an ice cube floating in her scotch, pushing it from one side of the glass to the other. When done with that task, she looked around for something pink. She passed through Laney and The Defense Secretary, and the furniture and books and such that surrounded them. Noting that they were in the Oval Office, not The Pink Room, she gave up her search. Still, she wasn't content to respond to Laney, so she revisited her scotch, finishing it in three long sips.

Laney and The Defense Secretary remained at attention for their Commander in Chief.

The President poured herself more alcohol. "Would you like a drink?" She looked from one employee to another. "Either of you?"

Both accepted.

"Scotch? Vodka? Bourbon?" The President was uncharacteristically generous. "No mixers, though. Don't be pussies." Her white trash background crept out.

"Vodka," The Defense Secretary answered.

"I'll have scotch." Laney mimicked her idol.

"Very good." The President delivered the liquor to her favorite pair. "Should we call in The Secretary of State?"

"No," The Defense Secretary said and tasted his vodka. "May I have an olive?"

The President frowned. "Is that considered a mixer?"

"No, Madam President." The Defense Secretary walked to the bar. "It's a vegetable."

"Then, yes. Help yourself."

"Thank you." The Defense Secretary plucked two green olives with pimentos from a tray stationed at the Oval Office alcoholic beverage center.

Laney drank at commensurate speed with The President. She wanted to return to the topic of Dylan. She wanted to assure The President that his gaffe, in letting the world know that he had directed millions of dollars to The President, was not a breach of the treaty. That he had donated out of loyalty, to help The President win, and to assist in Mitch's loss.

"Laney, stop thinking," The President ordered.

"Dylan's gaffe—"

"Please." The President flicked scotch at Laney. "Don't ever say *gaffe*. That's some stupid media-created word that no one ever uses. The same thing with *vetted*. Did I *vet* Charlotte Williams before I nominated her to the Supreme Court?" The President mocked the day's press coverage. "Were *The Great Heist* contributions a *gaffe*?" She licked at her scotch. "Who the fuck says *gaffe* and *vetted*? I've heard these idiotic words a thousand times today."

"Stupid words, Madam President," The Defense Secretary agreed as he ate one of his pimento-stuffed olives, whole. "Untrustworthy partner," he added, meaning Dylan.

"Not to beat a dead horse," Laney began, "but we did try to eliminate him—"

"Twice," The President interjected, "and we failed, miserably." She fingered another ice cube. "Here's the point, Laney. In essence, I have pardoned Dylan and his crew. I paid him $500 million. I agreed to this unreasonable treaty…Is the man going to tell all about my moon landing?

"No, Madam President."

"No?" The Defense Secretary didn't share Laney's confidence. "How do you know?"

The President's facial expression demanded reassurance.

"I just do," Laney fondled the ice cubes in her glass and spoke directly to The President. "He wanted to embarrass you with the contributions. But it would embarrass himself—and his deceased father—if he revealed the faked moon mission. He won't do it. Period."

"Senator McAvoy, will you accept the Supreme Court seat if The President nominates you?"

Mitch was presiding over his own press conference, in New York City. "It's not just The President's decision. I would need to be confirmed by the Senate," Mitch summoned another in the crowd.

"So, if you were confirmed, would you drop out of the primary and become a Supreme Court justice?" The young, gay, male reporter was flattered by Mitch's selection. And he admired, well, became hard, scoping the senator in his finely tailored navy blue suit.

Mitch put his arm around Karina, who instead of residing with the press corps stood at his side. "No. Definitely not."

The President whipped her rock glass of scotch at her pink flat screen television. She was alone, in The Pink Room, watching Mitch's press conference.

"I have the highest respect for the Court. Its role is equally important to that of Congress. And that of The President." Mitch slicked his perfectly pink silk tie with a stroke of his hand. "And I thank The President for thinking of me. But I have committed to becoming President of the United States of America, and I will proceed through all of the electoral processes, with one never-changing goal. To win, and to lead all Americans with loyalty, courage, and gratitude for their support and belief."

A pause, which the mesmerized reporters actually allowed. Then Mitch delivered his hundred-mile-an-hour fastball. "The President believes in me so much that she is asking me to join the Supreme Court…"

"Fuck you!" The President gunned her entire scotch bottle at the TV. The screen shattered. To compensate, she retrieved a new bottle.

The sound was inspirational. But fatal, and sad. The sight was bold. Sanguinary. It was carnivorous. The venue was historic. Rich with defiance and quick extinctions. A place of victory and one of defeat. The crowd, the horde, had been a maculation of the throne, the vibrant, and the villagers. At times, en masse, they determined fate. At others, a singular voice of destiny was heard. Nothing, in terms of the intrinsic barbarianism carried out in this majestic architectural landmark, had changed in the few thousand years of its existence. Just the players.

Today, an animal, a bull, lay dying with a spear in its heart. In years gone by, the victim in the arena was more often than not a human being, generally killed by another from his same species, not for any purpose, just for sport. For the dictatorial leadership, and also for his subjects.

Laney, courtesy of The Italian President, had front row seats in the Colosseum. The chronicled fighting ground that Rome re-opened for its originally designed murderous usage. At moments, had she desired, she could have touched the petulant beast or the flamboyant matador who sought its demise. The nearby relationship with the lethal display, however, was sufficient. Laney didn't require actual physical contact. And besides, though she appreciated the perk of the best seats in the house, she needed the ear of The Italian President—not the athlete or his prize cattle.

"The President sends her warmest regards."

"I can see that." The Italian President touched Laney's knee. "She could not have done better to show her," the man performed one of his phony word searches, "affection for me."

"And your country," Laney leaned in.

"And my church." The Italian President took a moment to

congratulate the matador, who had just finished the colorful waving of his cloth weapon. "*Bravo! Bravo! Signore Califiore.*"

The mob roared.

The bull's roar died.

The matador rejoiced.

The Italian President matriculated, conforming to all that his environment offered. He shouted with his people. Pained with the fallen. Pounded his chest and exulted with the gladiator victor. And he spoke softly to the American heartthrob, or deaththrob, as the circumstances may warrant. "Laney, does The President have a plan?" He brushed his tongue in her ear, a benefit of the necessity of having a private conversation in a rumbling, raucous crowd.

"Yes, sir, she does." Laney returned the tongue. "She will appoint a pro-life judge."

"That is the treaty. So she must." The Italian President needed to end their discourse with speed, for two reasons: the rabble would soon quell, and he wanted to engage in intercourse with Laney as soon as possible, at a different but nearby location. "Do you have a list of candidates for the Vatican's approval?"

Laney removed a small piece of paper from her bag. "Like Mitch's, all of their abortion views are basically unknown to the public." Laney drove her tongue well into The Italian President's ear, "We need the middle-of-the-road appearance until after the election."

"So The President doesn't anger her supporters." The Italian President maintained his lip-locking interlocution and took the list. He pointed to one of the names. "That's who we want."

The crowd finally died down, and the matador exited his stage.

"How do you know?" Laney talked normally.

"We already…" The Italian President searched for the right word, "…vetted him."

Laney smiled, prepared to set the appointment in motion… and to fuck.

“10, 9, 8,” The President decided to roll the dice, “, 7, 6, 5…”

An imminent rocket blast in Houston!

“4, 3, 2,”

It was unbelievable. The modern-day lunar expedition was happening today!

“1.” NASA’s leading boss’s voice crackled with ecstasy, his countdown completed.

A fantastic gush of red, yellow, white, and blue burst from the rear of the most magnificent space-traveling ship ever seen by the eyes of Americans and those abroad. Today, again, human beings were going to the moon.

# SIXTEEN

"I thought you hated golf."

"I do." Mitch leaned against a tree for no particular reason. "But I'm good at it."

"You're good at everything." Barkstone wasted in the hot Arizona sun. There wasn't enough room in the shade for both him and Mitch. "I guess that's why you bowl and play ping-pong too?"

"Sometimes." Mitch pulled a leaf from a branch, the closest one to him. "Sometimes just to have a little personal time."

Barkstone witnessed their circumference of emptiness, appreciating Mitch's need to be alone, even in the boring squander of a round of golf. The presidential candidate, and the media that traveled with him, had just completed a seventy-two-hour, five-state tour. Montana. The two Dakotas. Wyoming. And Nevada. All had been visited, stumped, and pumped. Town hall meetings with hundreds. Speeches in front of thousands. Rallies with tens of thousands. Mitch, and Barkstone for that matter, rarely had a moment of silence other than sleeping. He was determined to give the senator the quiet he desired. Mitch decided to chat, however, leaving the solace and cool of the overhead plants.

"Should it be Phoenix? Tucson? Maybe Scottsdale?"

"It's…" Barkstone had trouble seeing Mitch, the strength of the sun impairing his vision, "…Phoenix. The capital."

"Thank you for the fifth-grade social studies lesson." Mitch strolled away.

"You know what I mean." Barkstone ambled after him, the nape of his neck blistering from sixty minutes of direct heat.

Mitch stopped, satisfied with his new location. "How are the numbers today?"

"You haven't looked?"

"No."

"She's two points ahead now, Mitch. That's a large jump from where she was just a few days ago."

"She took us to the moon."

"Did she?"

"I don't know, but it sure looks like the astronauts are bouncing around somewhere in outer space."

"I followed up on all of the scientific data that Karina collected. I talked to many more astronomers, physicists…experts in every area of space travel."

"And?"

"Most of them want to be anonymously quoted, but they all agree that we can't possibly get men to the moon."

"So we have the same information we had before? Just more people saying it."

"Yes."

"Anybody to back up Chocola's account of what happened in '69? And the early 70s?"

"Not yet. But he promises to deliver film crew to support his story."

"Bob…" Mitch picked up a golf club, one with a rather flat head, "…now that Stella…" He swung the club. Barkstone jumped back. The white ball sailed a few hundred feet. "…has passed on…God rest her soul…" Mitch shook his head, disappointed that he didn't quite hit his mark, "…I don't have a choice to make."

"For what?" Barkstone followed Mitch, who walked a fast pace toward his ball. Secret Service, stationed everywhere about the closed golf course, allowed Mitch privacy, watching from distances, as Barkstone wobbled behind him.

"For my press secretary," Mitch yelled over his shoulder.

Barkstone wobbled and hobbled faster. "Your press secretary?"

"Yes, man." Mitch had almost made it to the green. "Don't you get it?"

Barkstone, out of breath, just arriving. "You want me, Mitch?" He was surprised. Proud. He was beaming.

"Of course." Mitch squatted with a new club, eyeing his next shot. Success, here, required skill. He stood, content with his plan. "Karina trusts you. Absolutely." Mitch straightened his body, positioning himself parallel with the ball. His golf club perpendicular with the tiny round item, he tapped it twice into the grass. "Step back, Bob."

Barkstone hopped, his quickest movement—a few yards away.

Mitch took a practice swing, and then struck the ball. As it rolled toward a hole, he again engaged in over-the-shoulder conversation. "So, I trust you." The ball fell into the opening in the ground. "Yes!" Mitch clapped his hands together.

"Very good, Senator." Barkstone clapped his hands as well.

Mitch spun around to face the reporter. "Very good?"

"Your, uh," Barkstone, flustered, pointed at the hole. "I am so, so, thankful." His eyes welled.

"This is an important position, Bob." Mitch sleeved his club. "Work needs to start now, you understand that?"

"I understand. Unofficially."

"This is a risk for you. I appreciate that."

"No, it's not. Really…"

"Sure, it is," Mitch made the discussion more intimate, putting his hand on Barkstone's back, just missing the blister forming on his neck. "Your loyalty must transfer from the paper to me…Not when I win, but beginning today."

"Yes."

"That means that you write what articles I want, and when I want them written." Mitch ceased contact. "And if I don't want you to write something, then you don't write it."

Barkstone nodded.

"And if you do that, when I win, you will become the press secretary…Fair enough?" Mitch's smile was charismatic, truly presidential.

"Yes, Senator, it is. You have my loyalty."

The challenge was minimal. The stakes, negligible. Two cards. The additions; one, maybe; several, possibly. A ten, jack, queen, king, or ace was tremendous as a first slapdown. The card that followed determined the initial value of the hand. If a deuce, three, four, or such came next, well, things sucked. If another face card was delivered, obviously things were great.

Karina choked, swallowed, considering the strategy, much of which had been taught to her by her late father, Thomas Kelly, a Teamster and, fortunately for the family, professional gambler. Thomas earned roughly $100,000 annually from his Atlantic City and Las Vegas ventures. He died, young, from a stab wound. Still, he provided enough for Karina's upbringing…and he was an important, loving memory. Karina gambled in her dad's honor.

"Hit." She slapped *C* on her computer keyboard, the letter associated with dealing another card to her hand. The game, at minimum, challenged the potential First Lady's intellect. In reality, it was a software video game, with no consequences. When Karina earned *21* with the next card, she shut the screen, elated with her victory. "Like father, like daughter. I love you, Daddy." The monitor pixelated with icons of Word, Internet, Screenwriter, Final Draft, and then cut to an empty, dark color.

Karina, nude, as she regularly was in her home office, left the swivel chair that accompanied her computer station. The next stop, a sumptuous intrapersonal hot tub venture. Water drawn in between her electronic betting. Karina half wetted her toes and ankles until she was satisfied that the temperature was perfect. Then she immersed the private areas so coveted by Mitch and, naturally, Barkstone, and so many others.

The nation's possible forthcoming lady-in-charge lapped herself in the luxury of silky tap water, bathing like an ordinary woman in a bubble bath. She soaked, scrubbed, and savored the pleasures of her jetted spa. She relaxed. However, when a buzzer sounded, she exited the soapy water. Karina, now not an ordinary American, had other matters to attend to, notwithstanding that this was a day off. Still, she resolved to return to the tub. Later, when permissible.

"Your favorite president. Who is it, Senator McAvoy?"

Mitch was in the middle of a pop culture-fluff question-and-answer session. At Phoenix City Hall. He was about to respond to an inquiry that had been posed to him at least three dozen times before in the campaign. He determined to make it interesting this day.

"Well…" Mitch removed his green and white striped tie, "… let's start with his wrestling career." He balled up the tie, "Can you guess with that." He put two fingers to his lips, "Don't shout it out."

Two people, in the sold-out audience of about four hundred, raised their hands.

"The man was a known trouble-maker."

Same two kept their hands raised.

"Anyone want my tie? I'm sick of it."

The crowd cheered wildly, hundreds putting up their arms. Mitch fisted his tie into the air, still grasping it, taunting his fans. The cheering escalated. Women running to the stage were halted by security, same as at a rock concert. The Phoenix mayor smiled nervously, anxiously awaiting the cessation of the unfolding melee.

"For you!" Mitch gunned the bi-color garment at a heavyset American lady. She caught it, but not before elbowing a neighbor in the chin.

"Sorry." She really wasn't. She breasted the tie and then inhaled it, consuming Mitch's cologne and his natural body scent.

"He did this same thing once." Mitch was back to the favorite-president question.

"He took off his tie, Mitch?" an audience member yelled.

"And more!" Mitch unbuttoned his jacket. "And he gave it to his constituents…Who knows the man?"

The group didn't answer. They just screamed. For minutes. And then minutes more. It was mayhem, as Mitch ripped off his suit coat and threw it into the audience. When they finally settled down, he continued, "He lived in a log cabin!"

The crowd screamed.

"He freed the slaves!"

"Mitch! Mitch! Mitch! Mitch!" They were on fire. "Mitch! Mitch! Mitch! Mitch! Mitch!"

The presidential hopeful put out his hands, asking them something. Maybe to relent on their chant, maybe to keep it going. They did as they wished.

"Mitch! Mitch! Mitch! Mitch! Mitch!" The mayor jumped in. "Mitch! Mitch! Mitch! Mitch! Mitch! Mitch! Mitch!" The local politician wasn't even a member of Mitch's party, nor were the city council, but they joined as well, "Mitch! Mitch! Mitch! Mitch! Mitch!"

Barkstone furiously scribbled notes. Radio pundits recorded. Television crews videotaped.

"Mitch! Mitch! Mitch! Mitch! Mitch! Mitch! Mitch! Mitch! Mitch! Mitch! Mitch! Mitch! Mitch! Mitch!"

There was complete insanity. Men removed ties. Woman peeled off outer clothing, anything that didn't reveal bras or panties.

"Mitch! Mitch! Mitch! Mitch! Mitch! Mitch! Mitch! Mitch! Mitch! Mitch! Mitch! Mitch! Mitch!"

"Ladies and gentlemen," Mitch finally interceded.

"Mitch! Mitch! Mitch! Mitch!"

"Ladies and gentlemen," he tried again.

"Mitch! Mitch! Mitch! Mitch!"

"Everyone. Thank you."

The crowd took notice, and unswelled.

"Thank you…But praise him. Not me."

The crowd erupted again.

Karina disrobed, stroked her hair with a brown-bristled brush for a full minute, then dipped her feet into perfectly warm bath water. A second soothing, bubbling experience was on its way.

"Lincoln! Lincoln! Lincoln! Lincoln! Lincoln! Lincoln! Lincoln! Lincoln! Lincoln! Lincoln!" That had been the most recent Phoenix mantra.

Mitch had artfully brought the chant to a conclusion. And now, the pop culture quiz resumed. A man with a blondish red comb-over asked, "Who's the best music group? Country, disco, R&B, rock, whatever?"

"That's easy. It's a three-way tie. Led Zeppelin. The Kinks. And Blue Oyster Cult."

"Male solo act?"

"Paul McCartney." Mitch pointed to the man, asking him not to interrupt. "I know. He was part of the Beatles and Wings. But he's the best. End of story."

"Female?"

"Two-way tie. Diana Ross and Barbra Streisand."

"Streisand?" The crowd, in parts, murmured along with the negativity of the questioner.

"Okay, I don't agree with the totality of her politics," Mitch shined brightly, "but she's one hell of a talent. Does anyone disagree?"

Hundreds applauded, minus only a few holdouts.

Mitch motioned to a green-eyed lady.

"Senator McAvoy, I want to tell you, you have my vote and my whole family's. You are a breath of fresh air."

The usual clapping.

"Thank you, ma'am."

"Here's what I want to know…Your favorite actor…I've watched all your movies… I've read the biographies written about you…I have a good sense of who you like…But I can't figure it out…Is it Clint Eastwood? Val Kilmer? Jimmy Stewart? Charlton Heston? Cary Grant? Gary Oldman? Jon Voight? Matt Damon? Clark Gable? Ving Rhames? James Cagney? Who is it?"

"Charles Durning." Mitch's response was immediate, and clear.

"Who?" A twenty-something yelled from the audience.

"Who?" Mitch responded. "Do you know who?" he asked the green-eyed lady.

"Yes, Senator, of course."

"How many of you know the incredible work…and life…of Mr. Charles Durning?" Mitch asked the crowd.

About half raised their hands.

"I know Charles Durning, Senator," a man with a neatly shaved salt-and-pepper beard entered the discussion, "He's a hero."

"He is." Mitch, invigorated, gave his reasons. "Charles Durning is a two-time Academy Award, four-time Golden Globe, nine-time Emmy winner and nominee. He won the Screen Actors Guild Lifetime Achievement Award. He has a star on Hollywood Boulevard. And I love his agent!"

"He starred in *Tootsie, The Best Little Whorehouse in Texas, Dog Day Afternoon, The Sting*," an older man yelled out.

"And *O Brother, Where Art Thou?, One Fine Day,* and *Rescue Me*," a younger soul added.

"I know him as Santa Claus," the green-eyed lady wanted to be part of the fold. "*Home for the Holidays*, right?"

"He's done much more than that." The man with the beard knew Charles Durning's greatest accomplishments.

"Yes," Mitch acknowledged him. "What is your name, Sir?"

"Russell."

"You are a veteran," Mitch knew.

"Yes, Senator, I am." Russell was for real. He had served two tours in Vietnam. The man exuded strength. No one was aware he was a year and a half into Agent Orange-caused cancer. This was a man of patriotic honor and family integrity. He understood what it meant to be a brave American.

"Charles Durning fought for our country at D-Day. In the Battle of the Bulge. He was shot, more than once…But he kept coming back…He was stabbed with a bayonet…And he never ran away…The man—and that's what he is—was captured by the Nazis, and walked the March to Malmédy…Everyone with him was killed, but by the grace of God above, he escaped with two other men…One of them was shot…Durning and the other carried him, in their arms…on their backs…in whatever damn ways they could…" Russell was weeping inside, but his face, his eyes, showed only will and determination. "Charles Durning is a true United States hero, Senator McAvoy!"

The green-eyed lady cried. The man with the comb-over, uncontrollably, joined her. As did the majority of the fellow Americans present. Mitch, with sincere emotion, scanned the room, seeking his father, decorated, in the farthest corner of the hall. The General nodded, in firm agreement.

"Hit me."

Responding to Karina's demand, a four was provided.

"Cool!" Karina splashed bubbles, then picked one up and blew it into the air. With a perfect twenty-one, she was about to earn $1,000, matching the bet she laid down. She needed to wait for the other Internet blackjack players to win or lose their hands, however, before the dealer's cards were revealed. With time to pass, she blew another bubble. It floated a few feet until it struck an oil painting of a spotted frog.

"Fuck!" a man with the username *Horseshit* blurted out when a king sent him past the golden twenty-one. In this game, the stakes were real and, accordingly, the emotions.

"God damn it." *Mayor O'Snatch* muttered. A nine brought his total to twenty-two.

"I'll stay," *Vittle Tits* responded to a request for an additional card. His or her hand rendered a clean twenty.

The virtual dealer, now through with all players, flipped over a five, adding it to the queen that had been showing. This configuration required the dealer to take another card. An eight was produced, soaring its hand to a sour twenty-three. This meant that Karina and *Vittle Tits* were winners.

"Do-you-want-to-play-another-hand, *Soccer Girl*?" A computer-sounding voice asked Karina.

"Yes," she answered, her word transcribed through a voice activation system networked to her monitor.

Cards were dealt.

"Good hand. Good hand." Karina fluffed more in the bubbles, arching her back, permitting a jet stream to better massage an area of tightness.

"What?" the computer voice inquired.

"Negative, Knockwurst." That was Karina's default language so the cyberspace dealer understood that Karina wasn't speaking to it.

"Knockwurst? One of my favorites," said a human voice.

"What?" the computer voice inquired.

"What the hell?" Karina yelled.

"What?" the computer voice inquired again.

A man motioned with his hand through the cracked door, signaling that he wasn't entering the private area of the bathroom, at least not yet. Karina jumped up from the tub, ripping a towel from the top of the toilet, wrapping herself in a single movement. The man, hearing her water departure, kicked the door fully open. It was Mario Leggetti. "Let's go, Karina."

"What?" the computer voice inquired.

# Seventeen

"As President of the United States, what have I done for you in the past three-plus years? Have I kept my promises of change that I made to you when I first ran for the world's most important political office? In my heart…" The President touched the top of her chest, "…I know that I have."

She looked from left to right. "Did I change our Social Security system? Yes, I believe I have. All of you, including my generation and those following, can count on a consistent check in your retirement years." The President nodded. It was time for applause.

"Did the economy change during my leadership? I think it has. Unemployment is down and interest rates are the lowest in over a decade." Again, it was applause time, so The President momentarily broke from her speech.

"And I promised to take us back to the moon!" Here, the applause would be the loudest. So The President stopped talking… and began thinking…but a sudden knock on her Cheyenne, Wyoming hotel room door interrupted her internal brainstorming and the practice speech she was delivering to a hanging suite mirror.

"Madam President." It was The Defense Secretary, "Let me in. Please." His enunciation was fast. Urgent.

The President, annoyed, took her time walking to the door.

"Madam President. Open—"

She turned the knob. "Is this important?" The President's cheeks creased.

"Karina Kelly," he was exasperated.

"Yes, that little bitch. What has she written now?"

"She's been kidnapped!"

"Really?" The President took The Defense Secretary's hand, "Do come in."

The President had pinked up the room, draping a pink sheet over the couch, and insisting on management's provision of several pink decorative items.

"Have a seat," The President referenced the pink-covered couch. "Here," she handed him a pink television remote control. "I'm sure this is all over the news."

"Of course." The Defense Secretary pointed the remote at the TV, a flat screen adorned with pink speakers.

The President snapped up a pink ice bucket and two pink rock glasses. "Get me the scotch, would you?"

The Defense Secretary was still trying to figure out how to get out of the hotel's house channel and onto a news station. On the screen, some obscure blond actress was explaining the movie options available, moving from the most recently released pay-per-view blockbusters to children's specials to porn. The Defense Secretary pressed button after button in a desperate attempt to eliminate this unnecessary information. Nothing worked, and the blonde just kept babbling.

"Turn off the volume, get me the scotch, and give me the remote." The President was eager to learn the details of Karina's abduction and, equally, to have a celebratory cocktail.

The Defense Secretary obeyed on all counts. The President, in one push, obtained CNC. She elevated the volume and allowed, as background noise, the reporting of a talking head. Another blonde.

As she unconsciously absorbed the media's version of the kidnapping, she asked The Defense Secretary, "So what really happened?"

Dark eyes. Provision of scotch. A symbolic toast. "Not much different than what they're saying. Dylan released a three-minute video of him boxing a kangaroo—"

"A what?"

"I'm not kidding."

The President looked at the television screen, and there was Dylan, in shorts with no shirt, boxing a live kangaroo. The filmmaker and animal were roped off in a pit of sand inside a gymnasium. In the background were blurred out figures, skipping rope, punching heavy bags, hitting speed bags, and shadow boxing.

Dylan slapped the kangaroo twice in the face, then got caught in the side of the head with a quick left by the marsupial. It was a nice whack. The kangaroo jabbed again, but Dylan ducked. As he came back around with a right hook, he yelled, "Don't worry. No animals will be hurt in this film." The punch grazed the kangaroo's chin. Then, the scene cut.

A tenth of a second later, The President, and all others viewing, witnessed Dylan petting the kangaroo, who was now resting in his lap. They were on the deck of a yacht, miles and miles of blue ocean and sky surrounding them. This time, the pair was alone.

"Similarly, Karina Kelly will not be hurt." Dylan caressed his friend. The kangaroo returned the affection with a lick to Dylan's face. "It's nice here, isn't it, Karina?"

The camera whipped clockwise from five to eleven o'clock, displaying Karina in an evening gown. She was handcuffed to a railing, but was otherwise unrestrained and appeared unharmed. "I'm okay."

Dylan, off-screen: "Let everyone know how comfortable you are."

"I am being treated well…He's got good food."

Dylan, off-screen: "Funny, Karina."

Karina yanked her handcuffed wrist. "Mitch, save me! Find me and save me!"

Back to Dylan and the kangaroo. Karina's image and voice were no longer being transmitted to the public. Dylan gave a final offering: "Mitch, we'll be in touch, but not with you."

Screen to a bright red, then a rupture into tiny primary-colored particles.

The President killed the volume. "Has he been in touch?"

"He has." The Defense Secretary refilled The President's pink rock glass. "With Laney."

"This is good," The President tasted her liquor.

"No, it's great. A public relations dream. He told Laney that he will only negotiate with her. He wants Laney to come get Karina."

The President finished her second round. "Interesting."

"Mitch, save me!" Breath.

"Find me and save me!" Breath.

"Mitch, save me!" Breath.

"Find me and save me!" Breath.

In forty-eight hours, a lot of things can happen. Throughout history, the occurrence of a single event has caused a myriad of monumental, and sometimes devastating, chain reaction of repercussions in the forty-eight hours following it. Congresses have acted. Kings have spoken. Religious leaders have prayed. And wars have begun. But neither The General nor Barkstone, in all of their storied dealings, had ever seen such a cataclysmic, if not bizarre, reaction-filled two days.

The disappearance of Amelia Earhart, the kidnapping of the Lindbergh baby, and the O.J. Simpson trial combined, in the totality of their spectacles, didn't profit from as much media coverage as this very personal matter, as it indeed was to The General and Barkstone, had in the last forty-eight hours. A king—from England—as well as two European queens had spoken. Congress had issued a proclamation. The Pope, the Dalai Lama, and scores of religious leaders had prayed. No, a war had not begun, but a marketing, publicity, and advertising campaign, from one end of the earth to the other, in a form and manner never approached, had been initiated—and was in full force and effect.

Thousands of blogs and websites were reporting; discussion boards on all, flooded with postings of Karina Kelly sightings, well wishes, and messages of politics, posturing, and perversion. Newspapers headlined the kidnapping, editorialized it, and featured it over and over again within the folds. Magazines moved up deadlines, publishing early editions so as not to be left out of the fray. Of course, every television network and radio station repeatedly covered the story, with angle after angle examined, manipulated, stretched, twisted, and eventually, obliterated. Experts were retained, offering their theories and hypotheses. When experts weren't available, celebrities—A-listers, and has-beens—were interviewed. They opined with thoughtful, but mostly irrelevant, words. Billboards everywhere pictured the missing, beautiful, and intelligent first American fiancée.

"Mitch, save me!" Breath.

"Find me and save me!" Breath.

"Mitch, save me!" Breath.

"Find me and save me!" Breath.

There was already a Karina Kelly doll! Dressed to the nines in an elegant evening gown. Singing for the arms of safety of her future husband, Senator Mitch McAvoy. The General fiddled with the doll's stomach, generating its cries.

"Mitch, save me!" Breath.

"Find me and save me!" Breath.

He tossed the Karina facsimile to the side. "Where's my son?"

Barkstone mulled over a half-eaten pickle on his plate. He and the General were in Mitch's kitchen, skewering the remnants of a light lunch and the hype of their loved one's disappearance. The only differences from the usual found in this McAvoy home: Mitch hadn't cooked and Karina wasn't present.

"Do you know where he is?" The General asked again. A second inquiry was out of the ordinary, but these weren't ordinary circumstances. So he allowed Barkstone some leeway with his pickle.

"He's here," the reporter answered.

"In the house? With us now? Where?" General McAvoy spotted the stainless steel stove. *Is he in there? How about the matching refrigerator? Or the dishwasher? No,* The General surmised. Then he considered the living room. A space as wide and long as most homeowners' entire residences. *Is Mitch lounging on one of the sofas in there?* A silly consideration, given that The General had been in that room only minutes earlier. *This entire thought process is idiotic. Mitch isn't here!* The General knew it.

"Listen, Barkstone," the man of war verbally positioned his thoughts. "My son is not in this damn house." The General removed Barkstone's pickle from his plate so the reporter could better focus.

"Sorry, sir." Barkstone nervously stood from his chair. "Here he is."

A figure appeared in an opening between the kitchen and living room.

"Dad, I *am* here. But I have to leave."

"Members of Congress, citizens of the United States of America, family and friends of Karina Kelly and my political opponent—but never my enemy—Senator Mitch McAvoy. Tonight, I speak to you from my most intimate of places."

The President was in The Pink Room. Though there had been substantial talk about it, the public had never actually been privy to this room. Cameras, until now, were absolutely forbidden.

"An outstanding reporter…a Pulitzer Prize-winning writer… A lady who elevates women to equality in our nation, the finest country in the world…A woman who challenges me…"

The President reached for pink…a lighter…she lit it.

"Take this flame, a light…a light to lead us to Karina Kelly…A light to lead her back to her future husband, Senator McAvoy…A light finally to bring Dylan Travant to justice." She closed the burning orange.

"Ladies and gentlemen…children…I know you all care, as I do, and are watching. I am committed to saving Karina Kelly. To ending the siege over her body and person. However, I do want to tell you that Mr. Travant is being reasonable."

The President needed to placate Travant, as, after all, his whereabouts were unknown, and he did have considerable leverage.

"He is negotiating with my staff, in particular, one woman."

Here is where The President's public relations wet dream, as defined by The Defense Secretary, lay: Her administration, using all means and resources available to rescue her political foe's future wife.

"I am unable, due to a confidentiality agreement with Mr. Travant, to name this woman. However, please, let me tell you, she is not only the most qualified to carry out this gravely important task, but she is a fighter. A winner…She is also a friend to Senator McAvoy and Ms. Kelly…She is going to meet with Dylan Travant, give him what he wants—I can't say what that is—and return Karina to her fiancé."

The President, in The Pink Room, was magnetic. Hard as this leader was, the world recognized that she was prepared to save Karina's life, a woman who, truly, couldn't be more adversarial to her. The ticker tallied. The race was fifty-fifty.

"Then, when this craziness is put to rest, we can return to the issues, and you, the American people, can determine who is best suited to continue to lead you in change and prosperity."

The masses listened, waiting…

# Eighteen

The woman was cute. Thin, but curvy, with a short sundress that slightly blew up in the wind. The man wore a top hat. His body was straight, but exhibited some muscle. The pair, however, were symbols, posted on a door, indicating a unisex restroom. One that could be used by both guys and gals. Laney pulled the door handle. This was the first stop, per Dylan's directives. Here, the hunt to retrieve Karina Kelly would begin.

With the door fully open, it revealed a new man. This man was alive.

"Mitch?"

He was searching an area by the sink, and didn't respond.

"Mitch, what are you doing here?"

He turned, facing Laney, but still didn't speak. Instead, with Italian leather boots, he back kicked into the ivory tile wall. After several hoofed thrusts, the tile broke and Mitch went to his knees. Laney followed. Together, they ripped apart tiles until they created a hole roughly the same size as the sink.

Mitch, still squatting, looked at Laney. "He likes holes."

"I know."

"Take a few steps back, Laney."

Mitch stood up, removed a pistol with a silencer from his waist, and fired two quick shots into the hole. The bullets shattered the two-by-fours that lay behind the tile. In tandem, Mitch and Laney kneeled again and began tearing apart the decrepit wood. A creaking sound that had nothing to do with their demolition activities alerted them that an intruder was entering the restroom. Laney sprung up, and in three steps met a middle-aged redhead, a restaurant patron who wanted to use the latrine.

"Sorry, ma'am, hotel security." Laney quickly flashed a badge, something she rarely carried.

"Excuse me." The redhead dug her oversized beak around Laney and noticed the working in the wall. "Is it something dangerous? Should we evacuate?"

"No, ma'am," Laney blocked the woman. "There's just a walrus trapped in the wall."

"A walrus? Aren't they a bit large to be inside a wall?"

"Well, this is a baby one. Sorry." Laney pushed her out the door and turned back to Mitch. "Did you find them?"

"Them?" Mitch glanced at Laney, then returned to his search. "How do you know we're looking for the same thing?"

Laney yanked a piece of wood, revealing a shoebox. "A phone?"

"Yup." Mitch removed the top of the box. Inside were two cell phones, one labeled "Mitch," the other, "Laney."

"I didn't know Dylan was talking with you." Laney took her phone.

"Until yesterday, Madam President," Mitch mouthed directly into Laney's ear, where a shiny, miniature two-way communication device was stored, "Dylan was only speaking to Laney." Mitch knew The President, among others, was closely monitoring Laney in her quest to meet Dylan and secure Karina.

"This is nothing more than a game." Laney talked into Mitch's ear. He had the same state-of-the-art equipment. She, however, had no idea who was on the other end of his.

"Military, Secret Service." Mitch read Laney's mind, "But this is no game. The prick has my fiancée."

"He just wants to beat you, Mitch."

Phone ringing. Laney's. She picked it up.

"*Want* isn't the best way to put it, Laney. Dylan *is* going to beat him." It was Serena Boll. "I am going to be your tour guide. Are you ready?"

Laney nodded. She surmised there were both sound and video machines in this restroom.

"Good. You have five minutes to leave this obscene restaurant and get to the corner of Tenth and Ocean."

"Gotta go." Laney darted out of the lavatory.

Mitch watched the door slam behind her. He, and the team watching over, waited for his phone to ring.

Laney raced through the dining area. She understood Serena's characterization, noting the waiters dressed as penguins and female servers, posing as owls. The bartender, an elderly man not staying within theme, sported a ballerina tutu and a hat, which most closely resembled a loaded baked potato. The cuisine, Indian and Malaysian, reeked of curry, and the floors and walls were painted a puke yellow. They were barren but for photographs of roosters and chickens. Laney's uncontrollable nausea, though, was fleeting, as she exited the front door in less than thirty seconds from her lavatory departure. The few patrons, less the redhead who left for a restaurant with a working toilet, hardly noticed her haste, wrapped up in the disappointment of their meals.

Cell in hand, Laney ran down a stretch of a Miami Beach road that bordered the ocean. Passing art deco buildings of varied sizes and bright colors, she quickly eyed each and every street sign she came upon. The evening was clear and warm, with plenty of sunlight still available, but her path was muddled with numerous vacationers and locals. Laney acted as if they didn't exist, weaving through them to the best of her ability. Twice she elbowed a passerby, and once she hit, chest to chest, a woman with double-D fake breasts. Her sprinting assault came to an end in four minutes flat when she reached her destination, the cross streets specified by Serena.

The phone vibrated. Laney flipped it open to see a text message. "See that bus?" Laney read the text aloud. She nodded, seeing a city bus coming her way.

The phone vibrated again.

"Don't get on it." The President and the others had heard Laney's words.

Laney rotated her head, and then body, checking for a signal in every direction. She saw nothing that sparked interest. The phone rang again.

"I said *I* was your tour guide," Serena directed. "Stop looking around, and listen to me, Laney."

"Okay."

"Drop this cell phone, run across the street, and go into the garbage can. There you will find a milk carton somewhere near the bottom." The phone went dead.

Laney, going against a red light and heavy traffic, bolted to the other side of the road. CIA, Secret Service, and FBI stationed in motor vehicles, boats, and aircraft closely followed her.

"Get out of the way." Laney showed her badge, for the second time that day, to a man who was attempting to throw away the remains of a taco. She nudged him aside and began tossing out the contents of the trash can. Miami Beach people were now watching.

Mitch waited, with no spectators, in the Indian/Malaysian bathroom. He stared at the hole in the wall.

Hands messed with the usual gook and junk of a garbage receptacle, Laney retrieved the milk carton. Carefully, she split apart the cardboard top and poured out the lone item in it, Another cell phone. It buzzed.

"Hello."

The curious observed her, surrounded by trash and talking on a prize stashed in a discarded milk carton.

"Hello?" No one responded. "Hello?!"

"Don't be so impatient."

Laney thought she could hear the double blink.

"Look directly in front of you," Serena commanded.

"I am."

"What do you see?"

"People, cars, buildings." Laney didn't know what Serena was getting at.

"I mean directly in front of you. Didn't they teach you to focus in CIA school?"

"The garbage can?"

"That's right."

Laney dropped the milk carton. She was confused.

"Well?" Even with a single word, Serena was condescending.

"Well, what?" Laney was annoyed.

"Well…climb in."

Laney knew she was serious. "And then?"

"You'll see."

Laney writhed her slender body, poked her head in the can, and then dove in.

"Wild! Nuts!" A man in a thong exclaimed. Followed by like comments from numerous other beach observers.

All The President's men—and women—were equally exasperated. They radioed local police for assistance in navigating the underbelly of Miami Beach. A hopeless cause, they acquiesced to themselves, given the obvious time constraints.

Once she was fully in the can, the bottom dropped out, and Laney slid several hundred feet into the city's sewer system. Things went from unpleasant to outright disgusting. She received a text. *Follow the path.*

"What path?" Laney said to herself. Then she noticed a dim light ahead, and she started to wade.

Mitch's phone played rock music, Dylan's favorite song, "Who Are You?" Mitch answered. It was Dylan. "Walk across the street to the beach."

"I'm waist-deep in a muck of shit and piss, following this goddamn light like it's the North Star," Laney talked, half to keep her overseers apprised, half to divert her attention from the sewage she was straddling.

"How far away is the light?" a voice on the other end of her ear-communication device inquired.

"It's difficult to tell, maybe a quarter mile." Laney gagged. "Maybe a lot more."

"I hope not," offered the same voice.

She gagged again. "Me too."

"Just think of Dylan's punishment when this is all over." The Defense Secretary joined the dialogue.

"Yeah," was all Laney could muster at this point, as the liquid waste had reached mid-stomach.

"Keep your head up," The Defense Secretary responded, "and keep us posted."

"Yeah."

The phone, which Laney had been holding at face level to avoid contamination, rang. Laney answered. "Yeah."

"You must be nearing the light now," Serena said.

"Yeah." It was now quite bright.

“Good. When you do, you will see stairs. Climb up, and come back to Earth.”

“Yeah.”

The phone disconnected. Laney continued wading, praying to reach the paradise of the light.

Mitch had heeded his order, delivering himself oceanside. He was the only person on the Miami Beach wearing slacks, a button-down shirt, and shoes. He stood out not only because of his attire, but also because he was a Florida senator running for President. The fact that his fiancée’s kidnapping was the foremost subject in the twenty-four-hour news cycle added to the spectacle.

The beachgoers, collectively, were uncertain how to react to their close proximity with this mega-celebrity. Understanding Senator McAvoy’s circumstances, but unclear as to why he was standing fully clothed on the beach, they all decided to let him be. Some muttered among themselves, others stared, but no one approached him.

Music again. “Who Are You?”

Mitch flipped open the phone. “Yes?”

“Take your clothes off,” Dylan directed, “Go into the water, and start to swim out to sea.”

Mitch stripped off his pants and shirt, pulled off his shoes, and raced in black boxer briefs toward the ocean, discarding the cell phone when he reached the shoreline.

There were gasps and chatter and nervous laughter. Some even cheered, though they weren’t quite sure why. This entire section of the Miami beach, star struck and confused, watched Mitch dive into the ocean and commence a trek to somewhere for no discernible reason.

About a half-mile stretch up the coast, another group of onlookers scrutinized a beautiful, but filthy, unknown woman disrobing on the sand. Laney was following her latest command. Once she had peeled down to her underwear, she trespassed into the water and embarked upon a fated swim.

U.S. Navy and Coast Guard boats were alerted to track the water activities, as were Air Force personnel, in both reconnaissance planes and fighter jets. All, however, were ordered not to interfere unless either Mitch's or Laney's life was in jeopardy.

Both good swimmers, the pair had quickly traveled well beyond the range permitted by local lifeguards. Buoys signaling dangerous water depths were ignored. Helicopters above, however, were granted the proper attention.

"Senator McAvoy." Mitch heard his name from a loudspeaker.

"Ms. Maine." Laney heard hers as well.

Flying overhead each of them was a military-green helicopter. The pilots, though, were not United States personnel. They were operatives employed by Dylan. Pliable metal rung ladders dropped from the helicopters. Mitch and Laney were told to come aboard their respective birds.

Mitch's ingress to the green flying machine was easy. He had been trained in such excursions. Once the ladder hit the ocean top, he grabbed hold, and was uplifted into the helicopter without struggle. There, he was met by Wang, *The Great Heist* director of photography and The President's largest financial contributor in Georgia. The copter then flew south.

Laney's ascent, however, proved perilous. Wind blew the ladder in different directions, making it difficult for her to grasp. She paddled back and forth, round and round, in a several-foot circumference, trying to clutch one of the metal pieces. The continual aquatic motion and turning was tiring, especially since it was preceded by an hour of swimming and running and mucking through shit.

Laney stopped chasing, and instead treaded water to allow herself to regain some energy. After a short minute, she was minimally revitalized and re-engaged her quest for the ladder. Seeing it only a few inches to her right, Laney leapt toward it. The wind sent the device directly at her, missing her hand, instead knocking into her mouth. Blood sprayed from Laney's face onto the ladder and into the sea. Temporarily disoriented, the CIA agent sunk to her eyes in the water.

Noting Laney's distress, a man jumped from the helicopter, a feat that would've killed most people. This man, though, was not even injured. Through an underwater surge, Mario Leggetti met Laney at her legs within seconds of his Atlantic arrival. He wrapped himself around her, resurfacing as two people in one. By the strength of his left arm and chest, he hoisted Laney to the ladder, attaching his right side to its rungs. The airmen above then mechanically pulled them to the safety of the helicopter.

An Air Force jet, dispatched to the site as Laney's life was thought to be in danger, was waved off by the woman. She blew a kiss at the pilot, though, thanking him for the concern. The top gun saluted Laney, privately reflecting on how hot she looked in her soaked panties, and maneuvered the plane north, opposite of the helicopter's travel.

The Air Force closely monitored the helicopters' paths. Unfortunately, they were heading toward Cuba, and about ten miles from that Communist country's coast, the Americans watched as Laney, again attached to Mario, dropped from the helicopter back into the ocean. Similarly, Mitch, along with an unidentified man, hit the water. All four were wearing some form of scuba equipment, including oxygen tanks. The helicopters, now in Cuban airspace, jetted toward the island. Those watching over were now unable to track the aircraft. And the same was true for Mitch and Laney—their miniature communication devices were either destroyed or rendered inoperable.

Nearly one hundred feet beneath the cascading waves of the Atlantic Ocean, Mitch, Laney, and their newest tour guides converged. They were joined in their journey by two of the world's most modern submarines. These micro, one-man, uniquely pressurized vessels could subsist at the greatest depths of the ocean, crawling the ocean floor if necessary. At all levels, they were undetectable by radar, and they moved with such precision and grace that they failed to disturb any of the salt water life that surrounded them.

Mario motioned to one of the submarines, advising that, somehow, he and Laney would be involving themselves with it. Laney held tightly to his back as he fished his way there. Mario clasped his hands and legs to the starboard side of the vessel. Aware of the human connection, the captain of the ship ignited its engine and decamped. Mitch's team followed suit, departing with their own submarine taxi.

Rifling through billions of years of $H_2O$, archeological artifacts, and some history still undiscovered by man, Laney witnessed hundreds of species of life. She saw hues of red, yellow, green, blue, white, pink, and other natural colors, in the fish they mightily passed. She experienced sensational creatures of vastly contrasting shapes and sizes, some with frightening scowls of teeth, others with pleasant, affable grins. She was saddened when the underworld trip suddenly stopped. Mitch was not.

Halting at a cave of sorts, Mitch greeted the land by blasting his unidentified guide headfirst into the muddy ground. Laney watched as her ex-boyfriend bolted off into the darkness. Mario, determined not to allow the same result with his captive, engaged Laney in an arm bar, gravely limiting her movement.

As the submarine captains exited their crafts, Serena approached. "Help him." She pointed to the man on the ground, who was having problems regaining his balance. As they tended to Mitch's victim, Serena turned her focus to Laney. "Don't worry, Mitch will end up where we want him." Double blink—and a few dozen of Dylan's crew appeared with automatic weapons.

"Is Dylan going to keep his deal this time?" Laney removed her scuba equipment.

"Doesn't he always?" Serena noticed Laney in her underwear. With a two-finger signal, Serena had a robe brought over to her.

"Thank you," Laney said, putting on the garment.

"Of course, Laney. We wouldn't want you to be without clothes in front of the world, like I was in *The Great Heist.*"

"What?"

Serena injected Laney with a syringe.

The knockout chemical was short-lived, meant to keep Laney unconscious for only thirty minutes. When she awoke, she had returned to a civilized world. Well, Dylan's civilized world—a yacht, sea location, of course, unknown. She was chained to a chair, speech obstructed by tasty sugar cane taped inside her mouth. With an emotion she had never felt before in her life—shock—she looked at her surroundings, and the people inhabiting them.

Then, Laney was seen by the entire world. Television screens, in every country with satellite and cable TV, went blank. Black was replaced by fuzz, and then an explosion of tints and dyes and contrasts. To ultimately reveal a close-up of Laney, restrained, helpless, in her chair. Then a cut to a similar close-up, of Karina, in the same condition. The camera pulled away, revealing Dylan, Serena, Mario, the entire crew of *The Great Heist*, and more.

Men, women and children from the United States, Canada, Great Britain, Italy, France, Russia, Pakistan, Nicaragua, Argentina, Japan, China, Holland, Australia, Mexico, Belgium,

Austria, Chile, Brazil, Singapore, India, Saudi Arabia, The Congo, South Africa, Cuba, and everywhere watched, with mouths open and eyes wide, Mitch, in his black boxer shorts blasted into the scene and punched Dylan squarely in the head.

Dylan shook off the powerful hit and set the rules. "Wrestling only, Mitch. And till death do us part." At that, Dylan shot a masterful double-leg takedown, bringing Mitch to his ass.

The President, in The Pink Room, screamed. "Holy shit!"

Mitch interlocked his legs with Dylan's, spreading his hips until he significantly strained his opponent's groin. Flinching in pain, Dylan lost control, allowing Mitch to tie the score at two-two by getting behind his former college teammate.

Dylan remained on his knees, palms pressed against the yacht's deck. The crew cheered when he reversed Mitch, again taking superior position. Mitch, however, in the very next moment, stood up and caught Dylan in a flying cradle, crashing the pair back down to the deck. This time, Mitch had Dylan nearly pinned.

Laney shook in the chair, trying every possible way to release the sugar cane from her mouth. Karina simply looked on, eyes gleaming, at Mitch's current besting of her kidnapper.

The world was on the edge of their seats.

Dylan arched his back and neck, drilling his head into the floor until his concave position permitted him to flip to his stomach. With that maneuver, he outstretched his hands, attempting to gain some leverage. Mitch, though, hit him with a brutal cross face, obviously breaking his nose as the crack was heard on every television set tuned in on the seven continents.

Undeterred, Dylan was once again able to bring himself to his knees. From there, he forced his way to his feet. Mitch, clasping the man's waist, worked with glistening muscle to prevent Dylan's escape. However, it was to no avail.

Both men, now standing apart from each other, eyed the other's position. Each remained in place. Seconds passed. Mitch turned to look at Karina. The camera panned with his vision. Her face radiated strength and hope. Mitch, electrified with God's most righteous emotion, shot in between Dylan's legs, elevating his nemesis above his head. And, in one extraordinary powerful movement, he thrust Dylan into the air and over the side of the boat. The camera followed the filmmaker's crashing, deadly descent and impact.

The world, its leaders and citizens, had just witnessed the greatest love scene ever captured on film. And then their screens went black.

Laney's shock hadn't ceased. In fact, it escalated when the screens in front of her went black, as she was watching the same scene as the millions of others. When Dylan removed the sugar cane from her mouth, she couldn't say anything. She was speechless. She looked around. At Dylan, Serena, Mario, and a few dozen others.

"Laney, remember, I'm the guy who orchestrated *The Great Heist*, and our little trip to the moon." Dylan stroked her hair.

"I…I…I…"

"*I* what, baby?" Serena double blinked.

"I…don't…understand…how you filmed Mitch fighting with you like that. How? Blue screen?"

"Roll," was Dylan's response.

The screens lit up with picture and sound again. Afghanistan. Behind-the-scenes footage of the moon landing. Everything was being revealed. The entire fake space trip, in quick clips, one after another. The bombing of the Afghan ground. The bulldozing, then the building and shaping and molding of the moon surface. The training of the astronauts. The direction of Dylan. All intercut with Dylan's and Laney's Internet business—and sexual interludes. And then, the killing of Charlie Diesle. Laney saw an elderly man firing a bullet into the astronaut's head.

"Who is that?" she asked.

"It was me." The General walked onto the deck. "We don't condone shooting up heroin."

"What the fuck?" Laney looked from Dylan to Mario to Serena to The General, and then back to Dylan. "Are you and Mitch working together?"

"Sort of." Dylan waved a finger, signaling all of the crew to go below deck. Only Serena, Mario, and The General remained. "Let's revisit old times, Laney." Dylan took off his shorts, displaying his monstrous penis.

"Dylan, I don't think this is the time or place."

"Shh, Laney. It is." Dylan ripped his penis from his crotch.

Laney jumped back in fright, and disgust. But she saw no blood, only the head and shaft of a rather long penis lying on the deck at Dylan's feet…and then, another shorter penis in between Dylan's legs.

"It's a prosthetic." Laney said to herself.

"It's all prosthetics, Laney," Dylan advised, as he removed his face. With little more effort than it took for him to discharge his phony member, Dylan peeled the work of the most talented and expensive special effects makeup artist in Hollywood from his head. In mere seconds, Dylan was replaced by Mitch. A different penis. A different face. A different voice. A different man.

"Whoa," was the only verbiage Laney could muster.

Serena stepped in front of her. Double blink—and her face was gone. It was Karina. Serena Boll, the little-known sexy Swiss actress, was actually the high school star athlete turned star reporter turned presidential fiancée. Just a chick from New Jersey, Karina Kelly.

Mitch kissed Karina, long, and passionately.

Laney watched, as her brain frantically scrolled through past events. It all made sense.

Mitch was Dylan, and therefore also Christian Ranieri. This is how he gained access to First American. To the Temple. To Luigi Punto.

But what about Punto?

"Why did you allow me to kill Luigi?" Laney blurted out. "If you robbed your own bank, why let your longtime friend be killed?"

"He wasn't a friend," The General answered. "He didn't know that Mitch was Christian Ranieri. He had long ago betrayed me, well before Dylan's death."

*Dylan's death?* "So Dylan was a real person?" Laney turned to Mitch.

"Of course. Your research told you that." Mitch walked away from Karina and began to unchain Laney. "Dylan was everything you thought. A great college wrestler. A money-making action filmmaker. A drug addict." The unchaining complete, Mitch escorted Laney from her chair. "But I was a better wrestler, a better filmmaker, and I never used drugs."

"Are you starting to get the picture?" Karina positioned Laney toward one of the screens.

There was Dylan—the real Dylan—in footage that looked as if it came from a home movie. Pill bottles were all over the floor, the remnants of cocaine were on a glass table. Dylan was strung out in a chair. He was filming himself, high, part of an autobiographical documentary.

The footage dissolved and faded out.

"As fate would have it, the real Dylan Travant died later that day. Karina—," Mitch paused to kiss his fiancée, "—was covering Dylan and his mansion for a profile in the first paper she wrote for."

"I found him dead," Karina stated matter-of-factly.

"Still, I just watched it on those screens." Laney referenced the several monitors on the deck. "Mitch wrestling Dylan. Did that happen years ago?"

"No. The fight you, and the world, just watched…it was Mitch fighting Mitch…blue screen and green screen made it look like it was Mitch fighting Dylan. But it was only Mitch. A smart Hollywood trick."

"Okay, I get it. You assumed his identity," Laney acknowledged to Mitch. "But wait, I saw you, *in person*, fighting Dylan in Afghanistan."

"Did you?" Mitch nodded at Mario.

"You saw *me* fighting as Spiderman." Mario flicked his wrist as the comic book hero did. "I first arrived to the party as Batman. When Dylan followed me into the kitchen, Dylan transformed into Mitch, and we switched costumes." Mario turned the floor back to Karina.

"So when I found Dylan dead from his overdose, I called Mitch. Dylan had previously told me that he hated Mitch…but that he also loved him. He said that when he died, he wanted Mitch to give his eulogy."

"And I have given Dylan the greatest eulogy he could ever have imagined. Instead of dying as a drug addict loser, he will be remembered, revered, in history as one of the greatest filmmakers—and thieves—of all time."

"Everybody has won," The General pointed out. "The American people. The Vatican. Dylan Travant. Babies. Hollywood. The poor. The media. My bank. Christ, even The President will at least survive."

"What exactly does The President 'will survive' mean?" Laney asked.

"Laney, I've allowed you to live. I will always be fond of you." Mitch stroked her hair. "You are indeed a patriot…And, you will be my messenger."

Laney understood. "The President…you want her to drop out of the race? You want her to resign?"

"After you speak to her, she will want to drop out of the race. But resign, no. She can finish her term. She just won't seek re-election because of personal reasons. Between the Vatican's gold and the $500 million that The President gave Dylan, I have enough money to fund about a century's worth of presidential elections."

"But that's not why she'll be dropping out." Laney knew it was about the moon.

"Correct." Mitch pointed to the sky.

"You'll never have an article written about Chocola, the scientists, and the faked Apollo missions? And you'll never let the footage from The President's phony moon landing be shown?"

"Laney, I am a patriot. The United States could lose its status as the planet's greatest superpower if the world knew we faked our moon landings."

"But if The President doesn't drop her bid for a second term?"

Mitch just smiled and gave a slight nod.

"So The President will have her legacy?"

"Yes, she will forever be known as an agent of change."

"And you? The man who stole the presidency—the greatest heist of all."

Mitch looked at Karina. "Mitch McAvoy will be the greatest American president to have ever lived…for things people know that he did…and for things that they will never know."

Double blink.

# KENNETH DEL VECCHIO

*The New York Times*, in profiling Kenneth Del Vecchio's Renaissance Man accomplishments, wrote: "As usual, Mr. Del Vecchio was larger than life." Kenneth Del Vecchio is a critically acclaimed filmmaker who has written, produced and directed 15 feature films that star 50+ film and TV stars, including multiple Academy Award and Emmy winners and nominees. He has recent distribution deals with majors such as Palisades Tartan Films, Universal's Vivendi Entertainment, Anchor Bay and E-1 Entertainment, with several other large distribution deals underway. Mr. Del Vecchio is founder and chairman of one of the world's largest film festivals, Hoboken International Film Festival. He also is the author of some of the nation's bestselling legal books, including criminal codebooks published by Prentice Hall and New Jersey Law Journal Books/ALM; he's also a previously published criminal suspense novelist. In addition, he is the owner of The Criminal Law Learning Center, where he has taught thousands of police officers and lawyers...And he is a former Judge, who also has tried over 400 cases as a practicing criminal attorney.

Kenneth Del Vecchio's filmography includes: *An Affirmative Act, The Great Fight, iMurders, Kinky Killers, Fake, The Life Zone, O.B.A.M. Nude, Three Chris's, Alone in the Dark 2, The Drum Beats Twice, Pride & Loyalty, Tinsel Town, Here and There, The Crimson Mask,* and *Rules For Men***.** In addition to *The Great Heist*, his novels are *Pride & Loyalty* and *Revelation in the Wilderness*. And his legal books include: *Code of Criminal Justice: A Practical Guide to the Penal Statutes* (national criminal codebook), *New Jersey Code of Criminal Justice: A Practical Guide to the Penal Statutes, New York Code of Criminal Justice: A Practical Guide to the Penal Statutes*, and *Test Prep Guide to Accompany New Jersey Code of Criminal Justice*, with numerous others in the works.

For more detailed information about Kenneth Del Vecchio, including critical reviews and press quotes, please visit www.justiceforallproductions.com and www.hobokeninternationalfilmfestival.com.